NEW MICRO

NEW MICRO

Exceptionally Short Fiction

Edited by

JAMES THOMAS

&

ROBERT SCOTELLARO

W. W. NORTON & COMPANY

INDEPENDENT PUBLISHERS SINCE 1923

NEW YORK | LONDON

For information about special discounts for bulk purchases, please contact
W. W. Norton Special Sales at specialsales@wwnorton.com or 800-233-4830

Manufacturing by LSC Communications Harrisonburg
Book design by Fearn Cutler de Vicq
Production manager: Lauren Abbate

ISBN 978-0-393-35470-6

W. W. Norton & Company, Inc., 500 Fifth Avenue, New York, N.Y. 10110
www.wwnorton.com

W. W. Norton & Company Ltd., 15 Carlisle Street, London W1D 3BS

1 2 3 4 5 6 7 8 9 0

CONTENTS

NEW MICRO

FOREWORD

For those who already love microfiction—exceptionally short stories—this book offers you the best of the best. For those just now discovering micros, this book introduces you to a true phenomenon in recent American fiction.

The phenomenon is that stories have been growing shorter and shorter, for decades breaking down the conventions of longer fiction. Many of the most talented authors in America now write micros, even as they continue writing other forms such as the novel. Why? Because micros capture what longer forms can't.

So what exactly does a micro do, or capture? To paraphrase one writer, a good micro hangs in the air of the mind like an image made of smoke. Another says micros can bring you to a point of recognition in a paragraph, then, foregoing any novelistic wind-down, leave you there suspended in that wonderful moment. It's been said that micros can do in a page what a novel does in two hundred; and, perhaps more humbly, that micros are as intense as poetry, because readers who like to skip can't skip in a one-page story. Some dwell on the literary form of the micro; others simply say it's a new way of seeing things.

This phenomenon didn't happen overnight. For decades, writers experimented with shorter forms that flourished in the medium of the printed page. Then one day, the unimaginable happened—the Internet arrived. These were made for each other, and became possibly the first tech elopement in literary history. Their marriage spread microfiction to new audiences everywhere.

One last word. Although micros are fun to read—an intrigue, a joke, a mystery tightrope-walking across the page—be forewarned. They also go deep. These stories matter, almost before you know it.

—Robert Shapard

INTRODUCTION

All of the stories in this book are shorter than 300 words. All of them explore their own *terra incognita*—uncharted territories—through stories told in new and innovative ways. Sometimes they blur literary conventions, in what Stuart Dybek calls "a continuum of infinite gradations that spans the poles of fiction and poetry, the narrative, and the lyric."

Intrigued by this, readers have been happy to dive right in. That readership is almost as diverse as the stories, as we discovered in our years-long search for micro narratives in online and print journals, individual collections, and smaller anthologies devoted to these exceptionally short story genres, by whatever name.

We chose the name *Micro* to recognize Jerome Stern's iconic *Micro Fiction: An Anthology of Really Short Stories*, published a generation ago. His book followed a trajectory that readers liked, that of stories getting shorter by half every few years, beginning with

Sudden Fiction with its 1,500-word limit and *Flash Fiction* at 750. Stern's book, drawing from a yearly contest, chose a 300-word limit. All of these lengths remain popular, but microfiction especially is emerging as the leading edge of exploration.

What have we found? These stories are small but not slight. They invite the reader to interpret the unfilled spaces. They are rife with implication, demonstrating that what is lost in explanation is more than gained through imagination. These works expand exponentially with nuance and detail, and resonate in the silences like the last notes of a cello.

In other words, these pieces are brief, but don't take shortcuts. Their borders are permeable. They are mysterious. The paths to them unworn. And here are eighty-nine eminently talented authors—some well known and others new to the craft—each with news from their own uncharted territories. For you to discover and explore.

PAMELA PAINTER

Letting Go

'm standing at the south rim of the Grand Canyon photographing florid undulating rock walls that drop to alarming depths. But it is almost checkout time at my hotel, and I want to take a tub and use all their emollients, a habit my ex deplored. When a young couple approaches to ask if I would please take their photograph, I want to say, I'm not the Park photographer. This happens to me everywhere—in the Boston Gardens, along the banks of the Charles. Always a couple in love—like this couple in their multi-pocket hiking shorts and sturdy Clarks. I let my Nikon dangle from the beaded lanyard round my neck, and take their fancy smart phone, heeding their instructions. "You were always a good listener," my ex once said, "but sometimes you have to let things go." I line the couple up in front of the Canyon's distant north rim, bronze wall aglow. I wave them to the right a bit. Joined at the hip, they happily sidle right, probably thinking I am a good photographer. Then I motion for them to step toward me for another photo. Unaccountably, they shuffle three steps back—and disappear with scrabbling sounds and tiny shrieks. Then no sound at all. I whirl around for help but there is no one in sight. On hands and knees, I peer over the cliff's edge, but it hides the floor far below. As if to assure myself that they were once here, I look at their photographs. Against two backdrops, they are young, expectant, with squinty smiles in the morning sun. And then a blur. Breathe, I tell myself. I set the phone on a wooden bench for someone to find. It is the only evidence the three of us were here.

PAMELA PAINTER

Help

The music decibel is at an all-time high, and the barback just quit. Benny's pulling beers, pissier than usual. He hates college kids but he hates yuppies more. He gives Denise the job of sloshing glasses clean on upside-down mops that pass for a dishwasher. The job sucks, but Denise is taking the semester off to save money for art supplies. Benny doesn't know this. As she lowers a glass onto a soapy mop and turns it around, Benny elbows her arm. "I'm timing them," he says, his gaze locked on *Gents*. "The girl went in first and he followed." He pulls another Bud into a cleanish glass. "The girl in the pink skirt?" Denise asks. She feels like she's screaming over the din. "Three minutes, maybe five, they're doing dope," he yells. "Any longer, it's sex. No respect for them who has to take a piss." Minutes pass. Denise pictures the girl's pink skirt hiked up, panties tight around her ankles. The guy's belt buckle twanging on the floor. "Watch this," Benny says, and muscles out from behind the bar, a door wedge in his hand.

Denise doesn't have to watch to know where he puts it. He's back and only he and Denise can separate the thumping of the jukebox from fists pounding on the door. "You hear that," Benny says, grinning. She nods, sadly. She hears it. Once she was locked in a ladies room, something gone wrong with the door. She remembers calling "Somebody?" It sounds stupid to her now, calling "somebody?" But finally somebody came.

STUART DYBEK

Initiation

The doors snap open on Addison, and the kid in dirty hightops and a sleeveless denim jacket that shows off a blue pitchfork tattooed on his bicep jogs forward beneath a backward baseball cap and grabs the purse off a babushka's lap. She's been sitting with an arm through the purse strap, and lets out a plea to a God with a foreign name, and hangs on. The kid gives it another yank, one that ought to break the strap. It jerks the old lady out of her seat.

"Hey!" I yell from a window seat, and a guy in a suit seated beside me fingering his cell flinches like I've elbowed him in the ribs.

Old lady in tow, the kid is already one leg out the door. The doors in the car, like the doors the length of the train, repeatedly stutter closed and open while on the intercom the robot conductor's voice of gargled static repeats instructions for disembarking.

I stand and yell "Hey"—I'll have that feeble "Hey" to remember—and someone else shouts, "Help, police!" and someone else, "Stop!"

and the kid punches the old woman in the face, sending her glasses flying. She lets go then, flung backward as the doors bang shut and the train slides off along the station.

All of us in the car, except for the old woman pressing her babushka to her mouth and spitting out bloody pieces of what we'll later realize are dentures, can see the kid racing down the platform toward the exit with a wild grin on his face as he dodges commuters, and his pack of buddies, who've been riding other cars join in running, high-fiving as they go, pounding congratulations on each other's backs, each one swinging a purse.

KIM ADDONIZIO

Starlight

Ten p.m. walking past the Greyhound station on Seventh Street. Bums curled in every doorway. Rita's high heels loud, the silence following her like a man with a knife. *Do what I tell you.* Until she's running, past the Jack In The Box, lit up, inside solitary men hunched over coffee, torn sugar packets on plastic trays, black girls in striped uniforms. The Embassy Theater posters, DAMES, TASTE OF PINK, a girl with green hair in the glassed-in booth reading a magazine, Madonna on the cover. Into the Starlight Room where Jimmy's supposed to be. At the round bar two men are playing dice with the bartender. Rita orders gin and 7 Up. The room is round, too, no corners, mural of the city curving along one wall. Cords of strung white lights blinking above her. Three drinks later she swears she's turning, points a finger at the Golden Gate until it shifts out of range. Turquoise glow above the painted hills. Out of money now. Slam of the dice cup. The carousel spinning her.

Her father holding her red coat and doll, plastic pinwheel she won at the penny toss. Blurring as she goes by. She lays her cheek on the bar, the reins loose in her hands.

KIM ADDONIZIO

What Jimmy Remembers

Girls in white stockings and checkered wool jumpers, round white collars, red bows at their throats. Birds in Saint Christopher's schoolyard—hundreds of them, black, spread out across the lawn in late afternoon. The brick wall of the steel mill on Dye Street he could see from the living room window, his father in there working, his mother in a shiny black dress coming in at dawn after singing in some nightclub, waking him for school. Shivering and dressing over the heating vent in the front hall. Dark-blue blazer and black shoes. A puppy that died of distemper, put in a shopping bag and into a can in Bushler's Alley. Cotton candy on the boardwalk in Seaside Heights, the barkers calling *Hey bub, Hey sonny, Buster, Skip, You.* Mickey the Waffle-Whiffer, old retarded guy they used to tease by dropping pennies into his coffee at the Meatball Cafe. Stickball in the streets. Touching Mary Prinski's left breast, just the underside of it, not even getting to the nipple but that was enough. The black hearse carrying his father through the snow, a semicircle of metal folding chairs. The green faces in avocado leaves smiling down at him. God in the clouds. *Who art in Heaven.* His mother, ghost now: wearing a stolen mink, flipping a cigarette from a deck of Lucky's. His father moving toward her with a match, cupping his palms around the flame.

BRIAN HINSHAW

The Custodian

The job would get boring if you didn't mix it up a little. Like this woman in 14-A, the nurses called her the mockingbird, start any song and this old lady would sing it through. Couldn't speak, couldn't eat a lick of solid food, but she sang like a house on fire. So for a kick, I would go in there with my mop and such, prop the door open with a bucket, and set her going. She was best at songs you'd sing with a group—"Oh Susanna," campfire stuff. Any kind of Christmas song worked good too, and it always cracked the nurses up if I could get her into "Let It Snow" during a heat spell. We'd try to make her take up a song from the radio or some of the old songs with cursing in them, but she would never go for those. Although once I had her do "How Dry I Am" while Nurse Winchell fussed with the catheter.

Yesterday, her daughter or maybe granddaughter comes in while 14-A and I were partway into "Auld Lang Syne" and the daughter says "oh oh oh" like she had interrupted scintillating conversation and then she takes a long look at 14-A there in the gurney with her eyes shut and her curled-up hands, taking a cup of kindness yet and the daughter looks at me the way a girl does at the end of an old movie and she says, "my god," says, "you're an angel," and now I can't do it anymore, can hardly step into the room.

SARAH FRELIGH

Another Thing

That year the heat started after Memorial Day and didn't quit until Halloween. There was no rain to speak of. The corn shriveled up and slumped in the fields like old men who had run out of hope. A woman who claimed to be part Iroquois read the sky at night and told us all it was our last summer on earth.

My mother said the world couldn't end without a party. The first Saturday in August, my father strung Japanese lanterns between the trees in our back yard. My mother rolled her hair and put on stockings and a dress that showed her thighs when she danced. I walked around collecting dirty glasses on a cork-covered tray. The women pinched my cheek and told me how big I'd gotten, like they hadn't seen me for years.

The party got louder. The women left lipstick mouths on the rims of plastic glasses. The men rolled up their sleeves. I hid inside the willow tree behind the garage and ate the melting ice from two glasses of

Scotch. I heard a sound like the rustle of grass before a storm, but it was only my mother's dress as she moved closer to Mr. Cullen.

"Marie," he said, like there was something he had to say to her. There was the liquid clear sound of kissing and he didn't say another thing.

Late in the night, I watched father lead my mother onto the dance floor. She fit her body into his and smiled up at his eyes, her teeth bright against her dark lipstick. Their feet moved together in dangerous perfect time. When they turned, I could see her hand on his back, her nails like red holes in the white of his shirt.

That was our last summer after all.

SARAH FRELIGH

We Smoke

We smoke because the nuns say we shouldn't—he-man Marlboros or Salems, slender and meadow fresh, over cups of thin coffee at the Bridge Diner. We fill an ashtray in an hour easy while Ruby the waitress marries ketchups and tells us horror stories about how her first labor went on for fifty-two hours until her boy was yanked out of her butt first and now she has this theory that kids who come out like that got their brains in their asses from Day One. She says we're smart to give our babies away to some Barbie-and-Ken couple with a house and a yard with real grass and a swing set, and we nod like we agree with her and smoke some more.

Nights we huddle up under the bathroom window in the Mercy Home for Unwed Mothers and blow smoke at the stained sky while we swap stories about our babies doing handstands on our bladders, playing volleyball with our hearts, how our sons will be presidents or astronauts, and our daughters will be beautiful and chaste, and because we know our babies are not ours at all, we talk about everything and nothing while we watch a moth bang up against the light and smoke some more.

LORRAINE LÓPEZ

The Night Aliens in a White Van Kidnapped My Teenage Son Near the Baptist Church Parking Lot

He admits being peeved, my boy does. Not allowed to sleep over with a shady friend with no phone, only a beeper, my son settles, enough to go to bed, earlier than usual even. But he tosses, twists—then pops the screen and leaps out, scrambling for the damp lap of grass near the Baptist church parking lot across the street. In the muzzy mosquito haze funneling from the street light, he considers *in-* words, like "injustice" and "inalienable rights," when extraterrestrials—two or twenty, he can't be sure—careen in a white Dodge van—brakes shrieking, tires thumping speed bumps—onto the church lot.

Laughing and scratching like their skins don't fit, they ask for directions to Peanut's Red Neck Bar-be-que, and my boy, ever helpful, points and starts to explain as they hurtle from the van, rushing him. They snatch him with long, spongy arms and slam him in the back. Then, tires wailing, they haul out to the street. Cramped between crates, he's still keen to an idea. When the aliens brake for a red light, he yanks the latch, spills out the rear door, runs like fire for the back streets. In an alley, he pulls a mangled girl's bike from a trash heap and wobbles home.

Because I'd locked his window after finding his bed empty, the buzzing doorbell jolts me alert. Shaken, he can barely speak. Says if I call the police, they'll *never* believe it. Shush, I say, hush. I run him a bubbling tub, press two baby aspirin into his palm, and finally tuck him to sleep. Now *I* twist and toss, pull the curtains apart to check for white vans, listen for the squeal of brakes, the awful laughter, *something* alien out there, ready to wrench my boy from me.

JOY WILLIAMS

Clean

A child in the south side of town was killed in a drive-by shooting. He was not the intended victim, he was only seven. There really was no intended victim. The gunman just wanted to spook some folks, the folks in this specific house. It wasn't even little Luis's house. But he was there, visiting a friend who had a pet iguana, and the iguana was sort of sickly, no one knew why, more yellow than green, maybe someone had fed it spinach by mistake. Hearing a ruckus, the boys ran outside and Luis was shot in the chest and died.

The family held a car wash to pay for the funeral expenses. This is not uncommon. It was announced in the newspaper and lots of people came, most of whom had nice waxed cars that didn't need washing, and the family appreciated this.

NANCY STOHLMAN

Death Row Hugger

For some reason it's always at night. It's always the same room, the light's always jaundiced. The room smells musty, like wet clothes were shoved and left to die in all the corners.

I guess I was destined for this job. My parents weren't the hugging type, so I've always had a malnourished craving for arms around me. I started as a professional baby cuddler for preemies in the NICU; each night after visiting hours, I settled into a wooden rocking chair with these miniature babies and their ancient faces and whispered of a future when they'd be strong and full-sized.

But nothing could prepare me for being a Volunteer Hugger on Death Row. You enter that holding room, and there they are, trying to enjoy their steaks or lobsters or Cuban cigars or whatever. My job is to hug them just before they take that long walk. It's not a sexual hug, though I have felt a few erections, and a few have tried to kiss me, but I politely turn my cheek and squeeze them harder. Because there's this moment in the hug, you see, where it goes from something awkward and obligatory to when they melt into my arms, weeping with their bodies. Every now and then I hear one whisper in my ear, and once one called me Mama.

NANCY STOHLMAN

I Found Your Voodoo Doll on the Dance Floor After Last Call

It was squishy under my feet and at first I thought it was a wad of napkins. But as the crowds cleared, it became obvious. It looked just like me if I'd been made out of cornstalks and had button eyes. *Is that really how you see me?* I thought as I picked it up and smoothed the yarn hair.

My first instinct was to toss it into the dumpster but I had doubts—what if it landed on its head? Was stabbed by sharp cardboard? What if I woke in the morning and found myself buried alive or impaled on a U-Haul box?

The mantel was out of the question, too far to fall if the cat knocked it down. A cabinet wouldn't work—there was suffocation, asphyxiation. Anything near a sink was out. Nothing near the fireplace, on the balcony, near a window.

A bird cage seemed the best solution.

One day I rushed home from work and the cage door was open,

the voodoo doll missing. I stared a blank, button-eyed stare into its empty depths.

When I saw you at the bar later, voodoo doll on a chain around your neck, I collapsed to my knees in front of you. Thank god, I said.

I knew you'd be back, you said.

STEVEN SHERRILL

Alter Call

When Reverend Smawley plucked his right eyeball out—the plastic one—to hold over the congregation, the church-honeys swooned. Half the backsliders, purse-lipped and guilt-washed, like they just eked out a church-poot. The others, whooping like no tomorrow. From the edge of the sagging stage, I heard everything clear as a bell. The tent went quiet. True reverence. Anticipation. Then a soft-wet thwack as the eyeball left the socket; that was all she wrote. Oh the weeping and wailing.

Besides folding chairs and passing collection plates, I drove, and played the organ. But—self-taught—by that time in the sermon, all I could do was keep up. Smawley stomping, hollering how "Jesus come down, as a piece of baling wire, and took that eye." When medical science filled up the hole with a worthless bauble, Jesus came back. Blessed him with *special* sight. "Come on! Look in this hole! See for yourself!"

Every night, his good eye patched, he gave the call. Sinners spilled into the aisles ready for miracles, even meager ones. Grocery lists, government cards, testimonials and prayer requests, offered up to that empty socket. Smawley read them all. "Go home," he'd say. "Take them little red panties off and burn them. B'leve on the Lord." "Turn away from that bottle," he'd say. "Towards Calvary."

I looked in the hole one time. We'd stopped for gas. I came out with two cans of beer. A bag of pork rinds. Set them on the roof of the Plymouth while I pumped. The Reverend, wore slap out from doing the Lord's work, clutching his thick bible, slept. Head laid against the window. That eye—open—gaped heavenward. I knelt on the oil-stained pavement, pressed my nose to the glass. I looked into that hole. I seen it all. You better believe it.

AMY HEMPEL

The Man in Bogotá

The police and emergency service people fail to make a dent. The voice of the pleading spouse does not have the hoped-for effect. The woman remains on the ledge—though not, she threatens, for long.

I imagine that I am the one who must talk the woman down. I see it, and it happens like this.

I tell the woman about a man in Bogotá. He was a wealthy man, an industrialist who was kidnapped and held for ransom. It was not a TV drama; his wife could not call the bank and, in twenty-four hours, have one million dollars. It took months. The man had a heart condition, and the kidnappers had to keep the man alive.

Listen to this, I tell the woman on the ledge. His captors made him quit smoking. They changed his diet and made him exercise every day. They held him that way for three months.

When the ransom was paid and the man was released, his doctor looked him over. He found the man to be in excellent health. I tell the woman what the doctor said then—that the kidnap was the best thing to happen to that man.

Maybe this is not a come-down-from-the-ledge story. But I tell it with the thought that the woman on the ledge will ask herself a question, the question that occurred to that man in Bogotá. He wondered how we know that what happens to us isn't good.

TANIA HERSHMAN

My Mother Was an Upright Piano

My mother was an upright piano, spine erect, lid tightly closed, unplayable except by the maestro. My father was not the maestro. My father was the piano tuner; technically expert, he never made her sing. It was someone else's husband who turned her into a baby grand.

How did I know? She told me. During the last weeks, when she was bent, lid slightly open, ivories yellowed.

"Every Tuesday," she said. "Midday. A knock at the door."

The first time, I froze. A grown woman myself, I listened to my mother talk and was back playing with dolls and wasps' nests. I cut my visit short. My mother didn't notice. She'd already fallen asleep.

The second time, I asked questions.

"Mother," I said. "He . . . came round. On Tuesdays. How many?"

"We are fallen stars, he said to me," whispered my mother, the formerly-upright piano. "You and me, he said. And then he would take my hand." She closed her eyes, smiled.

My father, the tuner, never took anyone's hand. He was sharp, efficient. I searched my mother's face for another hint or instruction. "Should I find myself one?" I wanted to ask. "A fallen star? A maestro? Am I like you?" But she had stopped talking and begun to snore gently. I sat with her, watching the rise and fall of her chest and the way her fingers fluttered in her lap, longing for arpeggios to dance across my stiffening keys.

JENNIFER PIERONI

Local Woman Gets a Jolt

It wasn't until lightning struck Michaela that she realized she married an idiot. She was running out in bare feet, to get the mail during a thunderstorm. August was full of storms in Porter County, but then again, so was Michaela. The rain and boom were terminal conditions, as were the flash and cracking of trees and Michaela's knuckles as she sat at the kitchen table with her calculator, ledger, and checkbook.

Her husband, Ron, wouldn't be home from work for another hour, Michaela realized, as she lay flat but electrified on the front lawn, which needed a mow. Michaela saw that the lightning lit the evening the same way the spark of Ron's cigarette lighters had briefly illuminated his face, after sex twenty years ago. She remembered Ron, in his prime, in his youth, with his flashy smile and wanted expression. With his bright girls, light girls, and twenty-eight positions out back of Mighter's field.

The pelting rain rinsed the thought from Michaela's mind. It washed over the grass and soil and, in time, would flood the basement, Michaela knew. As well as she knew the sound of Ron, down there, with the sump pump and a beer, cursing the cracking foundation of their home and God, for the August storms.

BONNIE JO CAMPBELL

Sleepover

Ed and I were making out by candlelight on the couch. Pammy was in my bedroom with Ed's brother; she wanted to be in the dark because her face was broke out.

"We were wishing your head could be on Pammy's body," Ed said. "You two together would make the perfect girl."

I took it as a compliment—unlike Pammy, I was flat chested. Ed kissed my mouth, my throat, my collarbone; he pressed his pelvis into mine. The full moon over the driveway reminded me of a single headlamp or a giant eyeball. Ed's tongue was in my ear when Mom's car lights hit the picture window. Ed slid to the floor and whistled for his brother, who crawled from the bedroom on hands and knees. They scurried out the screen door into the back yard and hopped the fence. Pammy and I fixed our clothes and hurriedly dealt a hand of Michigan rummy by candlelight.

"You girls are going to ruin your eyes," Mom said, switching on the table lamp. When Mom went to change her clothes, Pammy whispered that she'd let Ed's brother go into her pants. Her hair was messed up, so I smoothed it behind her ear.

"Too bad this show isn't in color," Pammy said later, when we were watching *Frankenstein*. While the doctor was still cobbling together body parts, Pammy fell asleep with her small pretty feet on my lap. I stayed awake, though, and saw the men from the town band together to kill the monster.

BONNIE JO CAMPBELL

My Bliss

First I married the breakfast cereal in its small cardboard chapel, wax-coated, into which I poured milk. Then I married a cigarette, for the gauzy way the air hung around us when we were together, then a stone, because I thought he was a brick or a block, something I could use to build a home. There was a bird, but flying away repeatedly is grounds for divorce. The shrub was a lost cause from the get-go and the TV gave me marital-tension headaches. The kidney was dull, the liver was slick, the car was exhausting, the monster in the woodshed scared the children (though I found his stink enticing). The teacup was all filling and emptying, emptying and filling. When I married the squirrel the wedding was woodland, the guests scampered, but all that foraging and rustling of sticks and leaves was too much. And the males sleep balled together in another tree all winter! How foolish, my marrying the truck, the shovel, the hair, the hope, the broom, the mail—oh, waiting and waiting for the mail to come! Marrying the cat was funny at first, and I luxuriated in his fur, until I heard his mating yowl, until the claws and the teeth, the penile spines, dear God. Forget the spider, the mask, the brittle bone. And then a slim-hipped quiet confidence leaned against the wall of the Lamplighter Lounge, chalking a pool cue, and I said, Lordy, this is for real. He ran the table, and I fanned myself with a coaster—this was going to last! I called home and divorced a plate of meatloaf. Confidence gave me a good couple of months. I learned aloof and not eating in public, but it did not last. He wasn't from the Midwest, and besides, tied to a barstool across the room, some drunk's seeing-eye dog was starting to chew the fishnet stockings off a lady's artificial leg.

JOYCE CAROL OATES

Slow

The wrong time for him to be returning home so she stands at an upstairs window watching as he drives up the driveway but continues a little beyond the area where they usually park in front of the garage and stops the car back by the scrubby evergreen hedge and then there's another wrong thing, it's that she doesn't hear the car door slam, she listens but she doesn't hear, so she turns slow and wondering from the window goes downstairs and at the door where there's still time for her to be hearing his footsteps she doesn't hear them so like a sleepwalker she continues outside moving slowly as if pushing through an element dense and resistant but transparent like water and at the end of the walk she sees that he is still in the car still behind the wheel though the motor has been turned off and the next wrong thing of course is that he's leaning forward with his arms around the wheel and his head on his arms, his shoul-

ders are shaking and she sees that he is crying . . . he is in fact sobbing . . . and in that instant she knows that their life will be split in
two though she doesn't, as she makes her slow way to him, know
how, or why.

NICHOLAS DiCHARIO

Sweaters

I fell in love with her beautiful sweaters. She wore a different one every day. Solid ones, striped ones, loose ones, tight ones, bright ones, white ones. Cardigans, pullovers, short sleeves, long sleeves, crewnecks, V-necks, and daring cowls. She reminded me of Aunt Rita. When Aunt Rita died, our family donated over four hundred sweaters to the Salvation Army.

She worked at the newsstand, this girl, in a narrow slot behind a glass counter, on the ground floor of a corporate monolith. She was a dash of poly/cotton color in a blue/gray blur of corporate uniforms. "Been meaning to tell you," I said to her one morning. "Love your sweaters."

"Oh. Thank you."

"Thought you might like to go out sometime, you know, just the two of us—cup of coffee, dinner, film. You remind me of my Aunt Rita. She used to wear sweaters all the time, just like you. Such beautiful sweaters. Her favorite was a Scottish cashmere. We buried her in it."

While I stood waiting, she sold two lottery tickets, *The New York Times*, and a cup of coffee. The security guard popped in and told her that he'd finished his screenplay and was looking for an agent. Then we were alone. She leaned on the counter, scrunching the delicate chambray under her elbows, and said, "Did you ever wanna fuck your Aunt Rita?"

"God, no! Of course not! Are you joking? You're joking. Of course not!" I often spoke without thinking. Bad habit of mine.

"That's what I thought," said the girl.

She turned away to sell a pack of cigarettes, leaving behind a trace of static, and we never spoke again.

MEG POKRASS

The Landlord

I smooth my hair, lean my cheek against the wall to chill. He wrote a note next to the emergency numbers, used the clown magnet, stuck it on the fridge. It said, for crying out loud, he's letting me live here cheap, letting me use his car, his CD player, his lotions. It's time. Says he's falling for me, even though I'm a walking disaster. Those words.

I walk out of the bedroom I rent from him. I pay on time. He's lying on the sofa, bare feet hinged over the arm. A dish of cocaine and guest spoons dainty on the coffee table near the fruit bowl. I bend down to tie my shoes, say, "Hey, turn on the Jacuzzi, I'll just run out for cigarettes."

He slices a sleepy-bear smile my way, my mouth stretches sideways and upward like a circus trick.

MEG POKRASS

Cutlery

I knew exactly what he meant, so I wrote my lover a letter in which I told him that I was getting good advice, finally, and that I needn't return. I knew he was without internet and accepted that he would never receive my message.

I asked him if he had been noticing the male store mannequins, as he did in the old days when we were falling in love. I asked him how things were going with the butter knife collection. My lover would duck into a kitchen store for hours. He didn't think there were any catalogs that would work for him, it had to do with weight and feel.

"They have lots of ideas," he whispered after leaving a kitchen store, smiling like a child at Christmas.

When I told him that to me, cutlery was not fascinating, but it was kind of maybe a bit interesting, he would glow as if he held a powerful secret. I would glow back at him and he would glow forward at me.

I had read articles about the way Chinese beetles mated. I'd watched videos of rattlesnakes having sex. We were each part of an intricate and delicate habitat, and we had our own ways of surviving. He had his butter knives. I had my dreams of finding a man who would find me.

SHERRIE FLICK

On the Rocks

Bob drank Scotch. Always. "On the rocks," he said, nodding to the bartender. He said it solemnly and because of that Sarah took him seriously. She came to believe Scotch was inherently somber, better than all other liquors.

He drank his Scotch slowly. This seemed ironic in years to come as she realized what he had wanted was quick and easy; what he had wanted was a shot of bourbon and a beer. He slouched as he crossed one thin leg over the other. When he smoked it was a long, thin 100. He lit his cigarettes with the lighter his father had given him for an eighteenth birthday present years before his father had died.

Bob looked rich and confident, and Sarah believed what he said over the slick bar top, ice clinking in his glass, smoke rising from the ashtray, the memory of his dead father resting deep in his pocket.

SHERRIE FLICK

Porch Light

This Monday, before her morning appointment with her therapist where she discussed enabling tendencies, Hayley ate spinach salad with slivered almonds, as she did every day. She drove cautiously just minutes before confidently telling her therapist she was carefree. Hayley always walks quickly—even uphill—but decided to not talk with her therapist about obsession. At least not yet. She bought new clogs and thought about kissing her next-door neighbor, Tim. Instead, Hayley talked to her therapist about her husband, Donny—his grating interest in sports, his strange, new beard.

That evening, after they finished mowing their adjoining lawns, drank a beer over the fence, and listened to Nirvana's *Nevermind* on her screened-in porch—Donny off at a baseball game—Hayley kissed Tim. The music reminded her of the irresponsible time in her life that she described as carefree. Back then she obsessed over happiness, but was usually discontented. She enabled a string of boyfriends, enjoyed dysfunction. Back then she wore vintage prom dresses to clubs, drank until she fell over.

Hayley kissed her neighbor who seemed to kiss her back, but then nonchalantly finished his beer, propped his hands on his knees, pushed open the screen door, and ambled through her cleanly shorn lawn and onto his without a goodbye.

Pretty cricket noises, pulsing fireflies.

The moon and yard sounds took over after Hayley clicked off the table lamp. Sitting in the dusky dark she heard a moth's papery wings clobbering the dim porch light. Hayley knew she'd talk of stability at her next appointment, of changing attitudes, of the need for a new monotone wardrobe and a juicer—a juicer with a variety of settings.

JOHN EDGAR WIDEMAN

Witness

S itting here one night six floors up on my little balcony when I
heard shots and saw them boys running. My eyes went straight
to the lot beside Mason's bar and I saw something black not moving
in the weeds and knew a body lying there and knew it was dead. A
fifteen-year-old boy the papers said. Whole bunch of sirens and cops
and spinning lights the night I'm talking about. I watched till after
they rolled him away and then everything got quiet again as it ever
gets round here so I'm sure the boy's people not out there that night.
Didn't see them till next morning when I'm looking down at those
weeds and a couple's coming slow on Frankstown with a girl by the
hand, had to be the boy's baby sister. They pass terrible Mason's and
stop right at the spot the boy died. Then they commence to swaying,
bowing, hugging, waving their arms about. Forgive me, Jesus, but
look like they grief dancing, like the sidewalk too cold or too hot they

had to jump around not to burn up. How'd his people find the exact spot. Did they hear my old mind working to lead them, guide them along like I would if I could get up out this damn wheelchair and take them by the hand.

BERNARD COOPER

The Hurricane Ride

In salt air and bright light, I watched my aunt revolve. Centrifugal force pressed her ample flesh against a padded wall. She screamed as the floor dropped slowly away, lipstick staining her teeth. But she stuck to the wall as if charged with static, and along with others, didn't fall. She was dressed in checks and dangling shoes, her black handbag clinging to her hip. The Hurricane Ride gathered speed. My aunt was hurtling, blurred. Her mouth became a long dark line. Her delirious eyes were multiplied. Checks and flesh turned diaphanous, her plump arms, gartered thighs. Her face dissolved, a trace of rouge.

I swore I saw through her for the rest of the day, despite her bulk and constant chatter, to the sea heaving beyond the boardwalk, tide absconding with the sand, waves cooling the last of the light. Even as we left, I saw the clam-shell ticket stand, the ornate seashore gate, through the vast glass of my aunt.

When does speed exceed the ability of our eyes to arrest and believe? If the axial rotation of the earth is 1,038 miles per hour, why does our planet look languid from space, as bejeweled as my aunt's favorite brooch? Photographs of our galaxy, careening through the universe at over a million miles per hour, aren't even as blurred as the local bus.

Momentum. Inertia. Gravity. Numbers and theories barrel beyond me. It's clear that people disappear, and things, and thoughts. Earth. Aunt Hurricane. Those words were written with the wish to keep them still. But they travel toward you at the speed of light. They are on the verge of vanishing.

BARRY BASDEN

Johnny Came By

He rode in on a little red Yamaha yesterday evening. Came all the way from Sacramento, took him four days. Said he stopped in Phoenix and my dad gave him twenty bucks for gas. Last of the big spenders that guy. He still owes me the twelve hundred he stole when I was in the army.

Johnny said he was pissing blood from all the road vibrations. He sat on the bike in the driveway while we talked. Mary Lou wouldn't let him in the house after last time. That was a while ago, but she's like that. He's still my son no matter what.

Then a grackle flew over and splattered him and it ran down behind his ear and into his collar. I hosed it off as best I could and gave him everything I had in my wallet before he rode off.

I stood out there in the growing darkness, listening to those fucking birds settle into the top of the tall cedar by the garage. I thought about taking the shotgun to them, but decided against it. Sure as I did, one of those paranoid dopeheads across the street would start shooting back.

BARRY BASDEN

Aerospace

Her ex lives in another state with another woman. Her new place is close to the beach. Nothing is familiar. Music pours through the thin walls. She hasn't heard so much bass since high school.

Saturday mornings she drives down the coast to Kelly's. He talks her into highlights then slowly turns her blond. She likes how his cut makes her feel sexy.

She drives the hills for hours, running through the gears, pushing the little roadster through the curves. Near Escondido, she parks in front of a cantina. Chalupas and squash gorditas with guac and salsa picante. Rosie and the Screamers and a stuffed horse in the bar. Wine margaritas and pitchers of beer. Giddyup. She wakes in a small room, a stranger beside her, a foul taste in her mouth.

Weekdays, she leaves for the plant in total darkness, roaring up I-5, nearly empty at this hour. She arrives in time to run two miles around the lighted track and take long hot showers before work.

On afternoon breaks, she shares a joint in Donna's van and buys junk food off the roach coach. An air force liaison officer, married, intrigues her for a few weeks.

Her father begs the doctors not to do anything else and goes straight from the hospital to the funeral home. After the farm is sold, her mother moves in with Aunt Mary. Her yearbooks arrive by priority mail, with a note in her mother's cramped handwriting, warning her again.

AMELIA GRAY

AM:103

Carla snapped the tines off the plastic fork with her thumb. "No matter how deeply I bury you in the gravel pit of my memory," she said, "you come crawling back out."

"There's no need for poetry," Andrew said. "I'm just here for my chair."

"I'm eating," she said.

"You just broke your fork."

"See, Andrew, that's just how you are. It's no damn business of yours how I eat, and what I eat with. What if I brought this fork to the door just to show you how serious I am?"

"All I'm saying is, you're not eating right now, and I want my chair back."

"I want those years back," Carla said. "I want my youth back."

"You may have your youth," Andrew said. He had a bag with him, and he reached into the bag and pulled out a small, carved box. He handed it to her and she held it with both hands.

"Sorry I kept it for so long," Andrew said.

Carla took a step back to let him in. "Your chair is in the kitchen," she said.

66:PM

"They're gold flakes," Wallace said, reaching to touch them on his back. "Genuine."

Tess held her hand against the textured gold on Wallace's tattoo. She drew her fingers back. "Are not," she said.

"Indeed they are. The artist was fantastic. He literally fused the metal to my skin, and I have to get it retouched every five years."

The gold leaf made a pattern of fish scales across his lower spine. "It's beautiful," she said.

"You're beautiful," he said, turning his head halfway.

"Not as beautiful as a gold flake."

He considered it. "Maybe not. It was a very special process."

"Must have been," Tess said. She felt sure she would die alone.

MEG TUITE

Dad's Strung Out Women Blues

The waitress plucked at her dollhouse features in the bathroom mirror. I was tempted to camp out in one of the stalls. Instead, I straightened my sunken shoulders and studied my strawberry tree hair. It was iron-red and stiff as a portrait. The waitress sniffed her middle finger, smiled at me, and sashayed out.

The sports bar stench of burnt brain cells and stale beer tackled the thick smoke as I walked toward my father. He was slumped in a booth, poured into his dollar-store jeans, unable to surrender to his declining choices and torn curtain of a past. His shiny face was a milk pool of Jack Daniels he'd sucked down through the decades that now snaked out of his cavernous pores.

The waitress pulled at her bra and stumbled over with a tray of forgotten nights. My dad and the waitress snorted and threw back a shot. She was another in a long line of tired notes my dad needed to strum. He always cried when he was drunk that he needed me. I figured out why as I slapped my wired hair against my skull and slugged back a beer. I was there to string all those painted smiles into some kind of demented tune.

TOM HAZUKA

Utilitarianism

I return home for the first time as an adult. My parents greet me traditionally, Mom worrying "that woman" isn't feeding me enough, Dad crushing my hand lest I forget which one of us survived Guadalcanal. But an odor of arrested decay has replaced the smells of childhood. The house of my youth is decorated with death.

Stuffed creatures fill the rooms. Local varmints predominate—squirrels, chipmunks, some possums and porcupines, even a bullfrog—but Dad hangs my coat on an eight-point buck, and the TV blares from the belly of a rampant and silently roaring grizzly. We stand entranced, almost touching.

"I bet you could eat a horse," Mom says, and bustles to the kitchen.

"You know Jeremy Bentham, the philosopher?" Dad asks. "*He's* stuffed. Mom and I are going to London to see him."

My father has hardly left the state since World War II.

"Your favorite! Liverwurst on rye."

Mom puts the sandwich and a glass of milk on the dining room table. Then I see that the cat I grew up with is the centerpiece.

"You embalmed Kitten!"

"Embalming is for graveyards, son. Mom and I fixed Kitten to be with us forever."

I can't eat with a corpse staring at me. "Where did you get all these, these *dead* things?"

"My God, boy," Mom says. "Open your eyes." A shadow nicks her face. "I thought you loved liverwurst."

"Your mother saw the ad in a magazine," Dad says, the two of them beaming as he puts his arm around her for the first time in my memory.

DIANE WILLIAMS

A Mere Flask Poured Out

The heavily colored area—it became a shade dingier—after I knocked over her decanter and there was the sourish smell of the wine.

I saw Mother reaching toward the spill, but the time that was left to her was so scant as to be immaterial.

The little incident of the accidental spill had the fast pace of a race, hitherto neglected or unknown.

"Go home!" Mother said. And I didn't look so good to her she said. "How dare you tell me what to do—when you threw me away! You threw your brother away, too!"

Within a month, Mother was dead.

I inherited her glass carafe with its hand-cut, diamond-and-fan design, which we now use on special occasions.

We do well and we've accomplished many excellent things.

"Don't do it that way!" I had cried. My daughter had tried to uncork a bottle of wine, but since I thought it was my turn, I took it from her.

Here are other methods I use to apply heavy pressure: I ask her where she is going, what does she want, how does she know and why. She should increase her affectionate nature, be successful and happy. Mentally, she must show me she has that certain ability to try.

DIANE WILLIAMS

Removal Men

You have people nowadays—the men in general, who were help-ing the woman—and that which they should not disturb, she had put into a crate.

She put a yellow-flowered plant into the crate.

The men's names were embroidered on their shirt pockets, but truly, there was no need to address one or another of them. A ques-tion could just be asked of one—without use of a name.

The pockets of their garments were needleworks with thread in bright white. But for Marwood, somebody had devised an orange and mustard-yellow embroidery.

The woman was standing a step aside and didn't have much to contribute, but she looked at a man—at what he was making ready to take—and she held her hands with her palms turned away from her body with her fingers spread, as if she had dirtied herself.

At the curb, the woman's car was an Opel, and the hood was up, and the door to the car was out, and what was its color? It was a butterscotch and a man, up to his elbows, was under the hood. Now and again he'd go back into the car and try the starter engine. Ted—that was that one.

It could be lovely, the woman was thinking. It was already lonely and there were mountains and mosses and grasses and violent deaths nowadays, and injuries and punishments, and the woman finds the merest suggestion of cheerful companionship and carousal—a bit too dramatic.

RON KOERTGE

War

He comes back reciting the poetry of war. Not that crap from high school, those stupid roads diverging. The real poetry of war. It recites itself to him, and he recites it back.

He'd like to give a rat's ass about the night school teachers and bartenders his wife has been sleeping with. He'd like to get all riled up and crash his new pickup. But he's busy listening to the poetry of war, which nobody else can hear.

His mother just sucks it up and cooks. His father is fucking hopeless. Crying when those buses pulled up to the Ramada two years ago, and now Dad's—what's that word?—baffled. Yeah. Fuck.

Then one day at the mall, there's this girl at the Hospitality Desk. Plain. Staring at a book maybe because everybody knows where The Gap Outlet is, and half the other stores are closed.

And he manages to put together a sentence. "What are you reading?"

"Something," she says, "sufficiently sordid to keep me from falling asleep."

Sufficiently sordid. Even the poetry of war stopped to listen.

Her nametag said "Ivy" and he knew, from a life before this one, how ivy could, in time, bring down any wall.

"Is that your real name?" he asks.

"What happened to your face?" she answers.

RON KOERTGE

Principles of Handicapping

A periodical called *Daily Racing Form* publishes past performances of every registered thoroughbred. Gamblers consult these brief histories to see how a horse they are thinking of betting on has performed in the past.

For example, a filly named Teen Age Temptress prefers weekends to weekdays. Past performances show that she tends to sulk and toss her rider on Wednesdays, Thursdays, and Fridays. Thus no savvy bettor would be attracted to Teen Age Temptress on any weekday afternoon.

I am a student of past performances, so am not alarmed when Sheila brings her revolver to the breakfast table on Sunday morning. She has done this before and ended up sobbing and penitent in my arms.

Still, there are always variables in handicapping. A sudden storm, for example, might change the track conditions. Or whispers from the denizens of the backstretch with new and startling information. I begin thinking fast since the grim set of Sheila's jaw is certainly a new variable.

ROBERTA ALLEN

The Beheading

We are driving through the bush in a jeep. I feel free driving through the bush, especially since I'm not driving. He's driving. The one his mother-in-law calls "The Dwarf." She doesn't call him "The Dwarf" because he's short. She calls him "The Dwarf" because his body is much too small for his head. I bet his head weighs half as much as his body, though there's no way to prove that without beheading him, which is not something I'm about to do. But it would be nice and quiet in this jeep if someone here—like his wife for instance—got the urge. His wife would be the most likely to behead him since she's the one he's complaining about. Everything she does, or did in the past, gives him cause for complaint. As a nurse, she probably knows the cleanest, most efficient way of beheading him, though that's probably not something they teach in nursing school. If I were a nurse, and knew how to do it, I wouldn't be surprised to see his head flying over the banksia and the scrub and the stunted trees growing here in the bush. Then I could concentrate my attention on the scenery. In the distance there's a sliver of sea.

ROBERTA ALLEN

The Fly

There's a fly in my ear. I hear it buzzing. It can't get out. It's not the only insect I hear buzzing. There are plenty of biting flies and mosquitoes in this tiny room, but fortunately, the others are not in my ear. The flies and mosquitoes come in through the open windows. We have to keep the windows open, otherwise we would die from the heat. I wake him up. There's a fly in my ear, I tell him at 3 a.m. He turns on the flashlight, takes a pair of tweezers from a case. Carefully, he extracts the insect, shows it to me. It's bigger than I thought. He goes back to sleep. But I stay awake, thinking about this fly in my ear. What would I have done if he wasn't here? Somehow that seems to be the wrong question. I have traveled all over the world. Never before have I had a fly in my ear. Why now? If I was alone, surely this wouldn't have happened. This happened only because he is here. This romance has made my head spin. I have let myself get carried away. Maybe that fly was trying to tell me something. Maybe that fly was trying to bring me back to earth. Do I sound absurd? Did that fly mean nothing at all? Is meaning only something we add on to things?

DARLIN' NEAL

Polka Dot

Maybe I wore a polka dot dress when I slid over the seat. If my panties showed, I wouldn't have thought much about it, just pulled my dress down when I got to the front, wanting the radio but we couldn't run down the battery. The parking lot was crowded with empty cars over gravel. We could see mountains bluish all around. I could hear the announcer in the distance, people cheering on the track. A man walked by carrying a folding chair. He had afro curly hair; he was white. He seemed sort of like a rich man to me, from somewhere else when he leaned to the window and asked me how old I was. I told him. Was it 11? My brother locked the back doors and fell over the seat beside me to lock the front and he breathed so scared as the man walked back by the car. "Don't look, don't look," he said as the man walked by and I glimpsed the man playing with himself as he slowed down, probably thinking he was crafty, hiding his limp dick from everyone else with that folding chair. It was hot in the treeless parking lot. All I gave him was my profile.

DARLIN' NEAL

Four Hundred Miles

There was always a coffee cup right there in the cab of the truck. The highway arced on through the endless sky, up toward the mountains. He knew a shortcut. He got out to open the gate, then he drove through and got out again to close it with respect for whoever might govern this piece of ranch land. He kept the radio off, waiting for dawn and all those colors, that feeling of waking up with the earth, and the animals outside. Crows speckled out everywhere, on the fence posts and over the grass. No one traveled the road alongside him except a prong-horned antelope who flew through the open distance and out of sight. Behind him, toward home, his babies were sleeping. His wife didn't need to worry about the landlord. The coffee cup warmed his hands. The long road took him away over the mountain, to work for a week and then he'd do it all over again. Unless he looked closer and saw the flick of the tail, or golden blinking eyes, the mountain lions high on rocks tricked his eyes into seeing nothing.

KEVIN GRIFFITH

Furnace

For days now, the furnace repair guy has been trapped in one of the ducts. How this happened, no one is sure. One minute he's inspecting the damn thing, the next . . . and because of the war, a war that never seems to end, I might add, the authorities are too busy to rescue him. Somehow he has positioned himself so that his face looks up through the iron grate of the main intake vent under our couch. Sometimes we slide the couch forward and let the children drop crackers and sliced apples into his open mouth. On certain nights, the children gather around the vent and listen to him tell fanciful stories about wolves, elves, and armless people. He needs to keep mentally sharp, I'll bet. I suppose that something will have to been done someday. Especially when we need to warm the house. But for now, we just have to get used to it—the smell, the snoring.

MOLLY GILES

No Soy for Joy

Joy can't find the soy sauce in her lover's wife's kitchen. She did not expect to find the nori, the mirin, or the wasabi, so she brought those with her—but soy sauce? Doesn't every kitchen in America have soy sauce? Her lover, watching with his beautiful hands clasped, doesn't know, nor can he help her look, because if he gets up from the kitchen stool she has told him to wait on, he will, he says, have to rape her. Joy smiles and shakes her head. Her lover is too gentle to rape anyone. Too gentle, too weak, and perhaps—she is just beginning to realize this—too stupid to make love without giving pleasure. Tonight he will please her in his wife's bed, but right now, hungry, it is Joy's turn to please him. She has already checked the cupboards. Still smiling, she slides the family magnets aside and opens the refrigerator door. Barbecue sauce, she mutters, scanning cold shelf after shelf, catsup, chili sauce, chutney, enchilada sauce, horseradish sauce, marinara sauce, mint sauce, pepper sauce, taco sauce, Worcestershire sauce—she stops. Swallows. Who is this wife clever enough to leave out the one ingredient that Joy's entire dish depends on?

MOLLY GILES

Protest

Two girls lie on their stomachs in the middle of the road, giving the finger to every car that passes. Most cars honk, but a soccer mom stops, parks her SUV, and crosses over. "What are you doing?" she asks the girls. "Don't you know you could get killed?" Her cargo of little boys stare out the windows. The girls slowly rise to their elbows, eyes blank. Both are thirteen. Both are beautiful. "Fuck you," the dark haired girl says. "Fuck you," her blonde friend echoes. A man in a pickup brakes. "What kind of language is that?" he shouts. "Fuck you," the girls say together, and put their heads back down on the asphalt. "You know what?" the man says. "You deserve to get run over." A gray haired woman with an Earth First! sticker on her Honda leans out and calls, "Are they protesting? What are they protesting?" "They're protesting being teenagers," another woman says as she jogs by. "Drugs," an old man decides as he and his golf partner roll up the windows of their BMW. "Everything's drugs," the golf partner agrees. "Or worse." The girls roll over onto their backs, arch, stretch, look up at the sky. "Please get out of the road," the soccer mom pleads. The blonde raises her middle finger. The brunette does the same. The soccer mom walks back to her car, gets out her cell phone, and dials the police. "Don't ever grow up," she warns the little boys in the back. But it's already too late. She glances in the rear view mirror and sees her own son's gaze slide away from her as he and his teammates sit silently, breath held, eyes shining.

STEVE ALMOND

Dumbrowski's Advice

All summer long, the summer of Dumbrowski's dying, you worried whether that waitress would sleep with you. There was always some magic sign. She smiled at you twice, three times if you ordered dessert, and her voice weaved musically through the unwashed forks and spoons. You admired her accent, she was local, a local girl, she knew where the rail tracks ran, swam naked in the stone quarry, held secrets in the hollow of her neck. You memorized her aromas—pie crust and parmesan, that lemony deodorant—you from somewhere else, a shipping clerk in charge of labels, auditioning for adulthood in thrift shop ties.

At the hospital, you told Dumbrowski: *I met a girl,* which might have been the truth from time to time, though really you dreamed of the waitress, your waitress, sweet greasy onion rings on her fingers as you lay in a pool of your own heat. Dumbrowski knew nearly everything. For three months he was your cigarette break, your boss, your father and you were his son and now he was surrendering to some absurd disease, gray as an old shoe, weightless, collarbones strung up like crossbows.

Once, at the counter, you saw her sip a chocolate shake, and it was almost then you worked up the nerve to speak.

He said you should live. This was Dumbrowski's advice when you told him about it, the way her tongue curled to capture that last speck of whipped cream. And you told him you would, you promised, as if you might know what that meant for both of you.

LOU BEACH

Humanity Services

Humanity services came around today. They checked on the size of our bed, the quantity of cans in the pantry, the amount of stretch in your panties. I wasn't home at the time, it was my shift at The Mill, and you were at work, but Angie let them in. They inspected her hair and teeth, measured Buddy's doghouse. Angie said they were polite. She offered them a glass of water but after testing our faucet, they declined.

LOU BEACH

Shot by a Monkey

Shot by a monkey, Elsa leaned against the banyan, held a bandage to the wound. They'd entered camp just before dawn, made off with a pistol, some candy bars, and a Desmond Morris book. We counted as six shots rang out, one of them finding poor Elsa's arm. Relieved that the simian was out of ammunition, we packed up. On the way out of camp we noticed a monkey on the riverbank, hammering at a snake with the gun.

STEFANIE FREELE

You Are the Raisin, I Am the Loaf

At 4:22 a.m. she crawls over the soft baby and onto her warm husband's chest.

"Am I snoring too loud?" He rests weak hands on her lower back.

"You snore big then he snores little. Back and forth."

He rubs his beard in her hair.

She tucks her knees along his sides. "Am I squishing you?"

"No. You're a raisin."

She reaches over to also hold a smooth baby foot. "Then you can't feel me. I'm so small."

"Too tiny. Why are we awake?"

"Thoughts. Busy raisin thoughts."

"You should try being the loaf. The loaf never stops thinking."

The river murmurs.

She hears deeper breathing again and speaks before he can fully fall asleep. "Are you sure I'm the raisin and not the loaf?"

"I am the loaf. The oaf is the loaf."

This must be his apology for earlier. She lets more of her weight ease onto his chest.

A few drops of rain drum on the awning. The few beats grow to many, drowning out the river.

"I don't need to worry about the big things?"

His breathing is even.

STEFANIE FREELE

Crumple

It was ridiculous, the back pain, the platinum white flash, the bent at a two-o'clock position, the grunting, the shuffling, the I'm-only-forty-one moaning. Just a Kleenex box I picked up. Only a squirrel I was trying to wave away from the bird feeder when the spine twitched again causing me to collapse on one knee, land on the baby's bouncy chair and slap my head on the toy basket.

An hour later they found me unconscious in a crumple. Donna, who stopped by to co-dog-walk, heard the baby screaming and opened the door. The same neighbor, an anti-kid woman—one who grimaced at runny noses—picked up the baby and held him until the ambulance arrived, until my husband showed up, grease-stained and wide-eyed.

Even though I was out cold, I could hear everything. It was a paramedic who suggested holding the baby to my breast. My husband told everyone to look away while he pulled apart my robe. The

taller paramedic said, "This isn't that weird, it's not like she's dead."
The short one said, "Shut the hell up, buffoon."

The baby instantly quieted so everyone could think.

I woke up and saw only the squirrel who hung upside down from
the bird feeder and chattered.

JIM HEYNEN

Why Would a Woman Pour Boiling Water on Her Head?

Why would a woman pour a pitcher of boiling water over her head while standing naked in a snow bank near a cabin in the north woods?

I was going to rinse my hair, she says, though we know there must be more to it.

See our woman with the flaming face inside the cabin now, rocking near the fire with a towel filled with ice pressed to her forehead. She was standing in snow when she burned her face, so she is trying to defrost her feet while chilling her face.

See a large stone fireplace with white-barked birch and sweet-fragranced cedar burning in a calm flame.

See a moose head from the 1920s pondering the scene from the log wall.

See old encyclopedias, magazines from the '40s, a piano with withered ivory.

See open rafters and a balcony with dark sleeping quarters overhead.

The room divides between moonlight and fire light, between pleasure and pain, between fire and ice.

Feel her burning misery, but hear her say, It is the mystery of the incongruous, as if this were enough to accept the skin on the bridge of her nose skimming loose like the film on stale cream at the touch of her finger. It is the mystery of the incongruous, she repeats, and offers a smile to all who will listen. I feel as if I have sinned, she says, and that I am being punished. But my sin, my sin, it was so ordinary.

ERIN DIONNE

New Rollerskates

Mrs. Peterson paid Margot a quarter every day to push the buzzer to the Petersons' apartment if Mr. Peterson came home early. Margot Twitter sat on the front steps of her apartment building, flipping the quarter over and over in her fingers, watching. Mr. Peterson was coming down the street, early. He was walking stiffly, as though he had Popsicle sticks for legs, and his hands were balled fists. Margot had been watching for Mr. Peterson for 160 days. She saved 159 quarters to prove it. They pooled, shiny silver, in a bowl next to her bed in apartment 5D. With the forty dollars, twenty dollars per foot, Margot was going to buy new rollerskates.

Mrs. Peterson was inside with Stanley, the building's handyman. Margot knew sex was going on up there. She chewed on the end of her pigtail. Her bedroom was right below the Petersons', and she knew that if she were in there she would hear the bedsprings creaking. Little groans, too.

She could see Mr. Peterson's red face now. He was scowling. Margot stood next to the buzzers, fingers lightly tracing the one for 6D. Mr. Peterson passed her in a surly gust of wind. The front door slammed. Margot Twitter took her hand away from the buzzer, pocketed the quarter, and sat back down on the steps. New rollerskates.

CLAUDIA SMITH

Mermaid

My sister killed herself the week I turned eight. Three days before my birthday. We didn't celebrate. That afternoon, I walked along the beach in my bare feet and filled my pockets with shells. I found some seahorses, but threw them away because they stank. I found a sand dollar. They were rare. My sister always found them but I never had. She'd told me once that if you crumbled them the right way, they would divide into pieces that looked like doves.

I crushed the sand dollar. The day was cold so I kept my hands inside my pockets, and just felt the broken pieces. I thought about the scar on my index finger, where she'd smashed a cracked shot glass over my knuckle. I pulled out the finger and kissed the white lines across my knuckles. She had a temper.

Her room was painted aqua blue. Not the color of our ocean, the color of postcard oceans we had never seen. Our ocean was gray, and on cold days, almost as black as oil. Only five days before my birthday, she'd walked along the water with me and told me that once she'd seen a mermaid behind some driftwood, through the corner of her eyes. She had only caught a glimmer, and had been afraid to look again. She knew the mermaid would either be beautiful or terrible to look upon. She liked telling me stories, she liked pretending Santa was real and she wanted me to stay a little kid. I told her I believed her. Then she asked me if I ever wondered what it felt like, to live someplace where there was no light, at the bottom of the sea.

CLAUDIA SMITH

Colts

We read books about colts, born in milky wetness, learning to walk, and then winning races. We knew what the Withers and Run for the Roses were about. The willow tree in her yard was our refuge, where our horses trained, and where our dolls jockeyed championship races. We tied our dolls to the weeping willows, swung them around like children on a carnival ride. I was thin; she was plump. Her parents had sent her to fat camps; my mother said her mother was the type to want a daughter in pageants. Her parents had cocktails and little wieners on cocktail bread with pale cheese. We drank the leftover liquor and fought over the glasses without melted ice. Our mothers didn't like one another, but recognized the value of girls and their secrets. Sometimes, we snuck into her father's desk and stole his letters. She never came to my house, but I told her about the loose change my father left on the dresser, how I took it to buy jewelry from the mall. Her father kept a stash in the liquor cabinet. My father was a cop. Her father was a lawyer. Our mothers both wore dark glasses, hiding their marks behind scarves and migraines. We compared their bruises as if they were badges. We tied our dolls to the trees by their necks. We hanged the cowardly women.

FRANCINE WITTE

The Millers' Barbecue

I t is the night of the Millers' barbecue. End of August ritual. Every-where, summer loves are shutting down. Sheets being draped over hearts like they are vacation furniture.

Mr. Miller, loan officer down at the bank, prods the burgers. They are nicely striped and ready to be turned.

Mrs. Miller glides through the yard with the same swimmy ele-gance she uses in their pool. Blonde hair and midriff top, she fills the glasses with lemonade.

Bret, the 19-year-old neighbor stares at her thighs. She pretends she doesn't see him. Pretends there were no late cricket nights in the garage while her husband slept.

While her husband dreams about interest rates and garden tools and oh yes, Margaret. Margaret, who is right now waiting by the grill for her second burger and ends each conversation she has with Mr. Miller the same way, "When are you going to tell her?"

Bret rattles his empty ice cube glass toward Mrs. Miller, who is talking to Frank Brown. *I am thirsty*, Bret whispers. And when she doesn't answer, he jumps fully clothed into the pool.

Where everyone suddenly stops what they're doing to watch this love-heavy boy sink straight to the bottom.

Everyone except Margaret, standing alone now by the grill, watching the burgers sizzle down to coal while Mr. Miller jumps in to save poor Bret. Bret who flip-flops like a landed fish once he is back on the concrete. And just as Mrs. Miller starts to look at her hero husband with an interest she hasn't shown in years, Margaret whispers into the burger-smoke air, "You know, *now* would be a perfect time."

FRANCINE WITTE

Jetty Explains the Universe

He starts like this: it's big and endless.

I point out that nothing is endless, and he rolls his eyes.

Jetty and I met years ago in an online chat room. We both had cats. Mine has since died.

Jetty was born Chester. Chester. Chet. Jet. Jetty.

He goes back to the universe. This is all the answer to the simple question I asked. *Where are we going?* It's a girl question, I admit.

"Who knows?" he says. He says we are floating matter, and no matter what anyone says, no one ever knows where they're going.

I remind Jetty of our two cats and how they pretended not to know the other was alive. Mine a tabby and Jetty's a Siamese. Mine got out and ended up dead. The Siamese wouldn't eat for a week.

"They loved each other bigtime," I say. "What about that?"

"They were just cats and therefore, totally random. Cats don't know anything," Jetty says.

"Yeah, well my cat is energy floating around in the universe. Right now, she is purring into your ear."

He goes to the fridge and pulls a beer bottle from a six-pack. I know the carton will stay there till I throw it away.

He pops the tops with his side teeth. Something I am tired of warning him about. He waves the open bottle at me like a finger. "Look, who cares where we're going?" He swigs long and gratified. "We're all gonna end up starmatter."

He likes that word, *starmatter*. He likes it so much he ends the conversation there. Finite. Done. Not in any way like the universe.

THAISA FRANK

The New Thieves

One night my lover said: you must learn to be like the new thieves—they never steal, they add. They enter rooms without force and leave hairpins, envelopes, roses. Later they leave larger things like pianos: no one ever notices. You must be like that woman in the bar who dropped her glove so softly I put it on. Or that man who offered his wife so carefully, I thought we'd been married for seventeen years. You must fill me with riches, so quietly I'll never notice.

The next day I brought home a woman in camouflage. She looked just like me and talked just like me, and that night while I pretended to sleep she made love to my lover. I thought I'd accomplished my mission, but as soon as she left, he said: I knew she wasn't you. I knew by the way she kissed.

I tried new things but nothing eluded him: shoes like his old ones, scuffed in the same places; keepsakes from his mother; books he'd already read. He recognized everything and threw it away.

One rainy afternoon when I couldn't think of anything else to give him, I went to an elegant bar, the kind with leather chairs and soft lights. I ordered chilled white wine, and suddenly, without guile, the bartender smiled at me. That night while my lover slept next to us, we made love, and the next morning he hung up his clothes in my lover's closet. Soon he moved in, walking like a cat, filling the house with books. My lover never noticed, and now at night he lies next to us, thinking that he's the bartender. He breathes his air, dreams his dreams, and in the morning when we all wake up, he tells me that he's happy.

THAISA FRANK

The Cat Lover

When a door opens and you can't see who's coming, it's almost always a cat that wants to be your lover. These cats take great care until one paw hooks and the door swings open.

After the door opens, the cat sits at a distance. It's the distance of masked balls, 18th century calling cards, once known by humans, never forgotten by cats. The cat stares in all its wildness and comes to rest upon your heart.

Last night my cat lover woke me from a dream where I'd been looking for someone in an unfamiliar city. The whole family had gone to bed in chaos: my son asleep by the television, my husband on the living room couch, my daughter in my son's room, me in my study wearing velvet clothes, something I do when I hope there will be no night. There was an unplanned feeling to the house, as though all of us, in order to sleep, had entered different zones and the house wasn't able to dream. The cat sat on my chest, but I shook him off and ate lemon ice that reminded me of a place in France where summers were so hot that ices dissolved when they hit the street. I stayed in the store to eat them and never knew what they looked like.

While I ate, I thought how nothing has skin—neither my children, nor my husband, nor me. Falling into his body was just something I did fourteen years ago, because light bound us together like gold. I finished the ice and my cat lover visited again: the approach, the encounter, the looming. His fur and my soft velvet dress felt the same—dark, pillowy textures, things to love and dream in. His small wild heart beat against my chest.

PETER ORNER

At Horseneck Beach

She's wearing a daisy-patterned yellow one-piece and an enormous blue hat and she's rubbing sunscreen on her husband's flubby back. He's got a cigarette drooping out of the side of his mouth, and he's so pale he looks like he spent the last thirty years in a basement. She slides her fingers under his waistband. He leaps and yelps, *For crying out loud, woman, on the beach in front of all these people?* She hands him the bottle. Now do me. He takes the bottle and squeezes a burble of lotion into his palm. Then he breaks an egg on her head, one hand cracks his lotioned fist, and he slithers both hands past her ears. She does not scream, just says quietly, I'll kill you you fat bastard. He shakes the remaining contents of the bottle on his own head and musses his hair. Now both have shampoo-lather heads. She takes his hand and says, I should have married Bea Halprin's brother, Aubrey, the dead one. *Let's swim*, he says. He'd have croaked by now and I'd be living on State Farm. *I said let's swim*, he says. They walk to the edge of the water and linger there. That wasn't funny about poor Aubrey, he murmurs, as his wife, who is Sarah, dives and shrieks into the cold June Atlantic blue.

GRANT FAULKNER

Model Upside Down on the Stairs

"A woman's beauty can be her damnation," her mother said. One guy told her he'd never seen an orifice he didn't like. Sure thing. But you've got to know something about tenderness. He just poked. She likes eyes on her, though, so she finds herself in the occasional awkward pose. Her boyfriend, the photographer. Her, the contortionist, the fucking astronaut. He'll have her hanging upside down from a tree tomorrow, his gaze going distant as his glory takes over. *Why doesn't anyone listen to me? Aren't ears an orifice?* The edges of the stairs wedged against her back. Never enough.

GRANT FAULKNER

Way Station

In Puerto Umbria, Maeve rented a room from a whorish-looking landlady. There was no door, only a wispy pink curtain. Her giggling brood of daughters kept slinking in to watch her dress and brush her teeth. There was little else to do than drink each night. A feline-looking boy in front of the cantina put his arm around Maeve and said, "Come in and have a drink," letting his hand slip down to her ass. Vultures ate a dead pig in the muddy street. She found comfort in the pink lamp's dirty tassels. Sometimes any kind of touch felt good.

LYNN MUNDELL

The Old Days

In the old days, there was no Human Resources. You worked or you were canned. Everyone took staplers and notepads from the supply closet. No one cared. In the old days, people helped you carry your boxes to the car, even Louisa, the manager you'd meet after hours in the closet. Although you were angry driving home, you wouldn't honk unless you saw a pal, like Ray. In the old days, people didn't flip each other off, unless you were Ray, Louisa's husband, yelling, "I got you fired, sucker!" People took the high road, except when they were provoked by someone who really deserved to have his block knocked off. It was just a shame that Ray called the police and your wife.

From there, life could go downhill pretty quick. Your brother would post bail. You'd come home to sleep on the couch. The years would begin to pile up like newspapers. You'd get another job, half the pay. You'd still wear ties, even when other men like your son-in-law started wearing babies on their chests. In the old days, it was okay to spank kids a bit. Except for your daughter Susie, they'd grow up fine, not bitter over nothing. In the old days, there were no "family meetings" with words like "behavior" and "concerned." You had family dinners, everyone, together. There was no Berkshire, A Skilled Living Solution. Old people lived with family. In the old days, I lived with all of you.

NIN ANDREWS

The Orgasm Needs a Photo of Herself

Preferably a head shot to go with a short bio. She takes a selfie leaning against a tree, looking too posed, looking not at all *au naturel* as she'd planned. She takes another selfie sitting on the hood of her car, smiling. Behind her, written on the front window's condensation, is her message to the world. She throws them both away. Then she lets her hair cover her eyes and mouth and tries again. She doesn't want everyone to know what she looks like. No orgasm does. There is a rule against an orgasm who shows too much in public. A rule against an orgasm who shows too much in private, too. Who lets anyone gaze into her soft brown eyes.

NIN ANDREWS

The Orgasm Thinks You Have Forgotten Her

That you no longer feel her like a tingle, a tug, or a whispered word in the back of your mind. That you have taken from her whatever you wished, whatever you wanted, whatever you thought you must have. And you have tossed her aside without looking back.

It happened so easily, she sighs—as easily as pulling a thread from a hem, unraveling her slowly at first, then faster and faster. Now she wakes, late and alone, with a memory of all she has lost. All that once shaped the hours around her like a lit and shimmering gown.

WILLIAM WALSH

So Much Love in the Room

The baby would fix everything. The baby would be a magic bullet. Their marriage wouldn't fail with a baby in the house. They would have more than a marriage, with a baby. They would have a family. Their family would not fail. They hated failure more than they hated each other, so they would do anything to keep their marriage from failing. They would have a baby.

Their gripes were valid. Their gripes were identical. They always agreed on this, their gripes. And everybody wanted them to fail, to stop succeeding. They were certain.

So they had a baby boy and they named him Beef and they dressed him like a clown until he was three and was able to take off his clown clothes and tell them that he wanted to be dressed like a farmer.

"One night," they tell him, sounding—they knew—too rehearsed. "One special night. We'll never forget. One night when there was so much love in the room."

ARLENE ANG

Unannounced Guest

The day we buried my sister, Mimi came. The rings on her face dangled. Everyone watched her as fish would observe a hook without the bait. She wanted to have the cookbooks that she had left my sister. I understood for the first time the word "lover."

Mimi stood there and chewed gum: *You got to admit there's something eerie about all these people who never knew her. And are here now.*

It was April. Dead fish were washing up from the lake. There are smells you bring home that write themselves into a novel. In this scene, I was serving egg sandwiches. I was thinking about the hour on Mimi's digital wristwatch—15:39—and how it created a private neighborhood peopled with silence.

My sister's husband stood apart, holding their two children by the wrists. There was so much sun coming in through the French windows that I finally understood the concept behind alien abduction.

RON WALLACE

Siding

You ain't got no vapor barrier in the house," the fat tin man wheezes. "That's what makes all your paint pop off. Now aluminum," he sings, "aluminum..."

The wife knows this song by heart, her song—the fascia and soffits and weep holes, the Styrofoam insulation, the window wraps and tracks. The stereo booms from the living room. "Just can it," she yells at their teenage daughter, her ears caulked with rock music.

"It's guaranteed," the tin man intones, "for life."

The husband isn't so sure. He thinks it's a surface problem—bad preparation, warped boards, cheap paint. He kicks at the family cat who yowls tinnily and bares her rotting teeth.

The tin man agrees, but says stripping down to bare wood is a bitch, and possibly an environmental hazard. Again, he counsels replacement.

The daughter, thin as a paint chip, wired to her walkman, scrapes the cat off the floor and peels out of the house, siding with no one.

The tin man continues—no rotting, no peeling, no blistering: a new start.

The wife likes the idea and picks and picks at the paint.

"Don't!" the husband commands her, watching his whole house flake slowly away, his old angers condensing, his face moist, his passion stirring.

His voice is as insidious as mildew, the wife thinks, lifting her hand like a barrier, her skin a nest of ants, her smile a stain on her face.

The tin man comes between them with his lifetime guarantee.

But things are getting steamy now. "Who asked you?" they say, cutting him off, nailing him firmly in place.

RON WALLACE

No Answer

f only she hadn't been so pink and steamy. I think that was it, the
pink and the steam, the glow of her nude body in the tub as she
lay gazing somewhere beyond me, the way women who should wear
glasses, but don't, look through you dreamily. Perhaps it was the pink
and the steam and the heat in the white-tiled bathroom, our five-year-
old daughter, Jennifer, sitting on the edge of the closed toilet, watching us watch each other, saying, "Mommy's naked, Daddy. Why are
you staring?"

The phone in the bedroom was ringing. It was Andrea. She was
calling from the cabin she'd rented in the Adirondacks, to see if I
could get free. After twenty-five years she'd written me from Paris
to say she loved me after all, and she'd be in the States this weekend.
For twenty-five years I'd dreamed of her, and how the full moon had
shown through the open back window of my father's old Ford on her
small breasts. And now she was back, wanting me.

"The phone's ringing," my daughter said.

"Aren't you going to answer it?" my wife smiled dreamily.

"Yes," I said, mesmerized by the steamy scene, the glow of her blurred nudity.

"Wash my back," she pouted.

The phone rang on through the pink and the steam and the old Ford and the moon.

"Now beat it, you big buffoon," she laughed, "so I can get out of the tub."

"Beat it," my daughter crooned.

I stood in the drafty hallway, musing. What was I doing? The phone rang on, desire still fast in its cradle.

When Christine stepped out in the hall fully clothed, her mouth in its thin set line, her languor and loveliness gone, our daughter hard behind her, the phone stopped ringing. And the phone rang on.

KIM CHINQUEE

No One Was with Him

He had his own business and let himself off at five, like a regular employee, and every day afterwards he called her, and today when she asked him how his day was he said fine except for the accident. She said what accident? He'd rolled his truck a few times. She said are you okay and he was fine, so he said he was perfectly fine. His truck was probably totaled, so he said that, and he wouldn't find out for sure until the weekend. She asked if he was scared and he didn't have time to be scared, so he told her that, and she said, but weren't you? Like, didn't you have a moment of freakiness? and he said no. He'd slipped his truck on ice, whirling and spinning, rolling one, two, he wasn't sure how many times, so he told her that. She said was your brother with you? Maybe your new puppy? No, Hun. No one was with him. Someone called 911, and she kept asking him more questions, like what now? and what if? and he felt fine, so he told her he was fine, he said he was perfectly fine, and she asked more questions and he heard something like some ripping, and he said are you okay? He pictured her bedraggled, her hair a mess, her naked, asking him again will you ever touch me, will you again ever, and will you, will you, will you? ever, do you love me? She said please and are you sure that you're okay and he said he was fine, Hun, he was perfectly fine, Hun, he was perfectly fine with everything.

KIM CHINQUEE

He Was on the Second Floor

They sat on the edge of the bed, and he let the dog up. She moved closer to him and he told the dog he loved him.

He said, "What're you thinking?"

She said, "We haven't had sex in months."

He laughed and she didn't. Then he said sorry.

"You look away," she said.

"Sex is just an act," he said. He petted the dog. The dog licked the sheets.

She saw lights on the highway. Whatever it was, it was speeding.

"An act?" she said. "Then why don't we just fuck? Let's have sex with strangers?"

She wanted to make love. He said he didn't know how. They'd already been over this.

He wrestled with the dog, letting it bite. He got on the floor with the dog, growling and panting with it.

She went to the kitchen to fix herself a sandwich. When she went back up, he was sleeping with the dog. There was drool on his arm.

ANTHONY TOGNAZZINI

I Carry a Hammer in My Pocket for Occasions Such as These

A guy I didn't like approached me on the street. He was wearing a backwards baseball cap and cream colored jeans. He might have said Hey man howzitgoing? He might have said Where you headin' or You aren't going to believe what happened to me today. I cast him a glance that read rapacious hatred.

He said, "You know why you don't like me, man?"

I said, "Lay it on me."

He said, "The reason you don't like me is because you don't like yourself."

I said, "Is that so?"

He said, "Yeah, perhaps a little sensitivity on your part."

I said, "You think?"

He said, "Yeah, we project onto others our deepest fears and self-loathing."

"You may be right," I said, considering.

We walked awhile together on the street in silence, buses rushing past us. I thought about it. He was right. I knew he was right. After a time the guy asked if he could borrow some money from me. "No problem," I said, and reached in my pocket for the hammer.

AMY L. CLARK

Looking for Nick Westlund on the MBTA

Now that boy was amazing. He was a bike messenger but he fancied himself a Picasso, and he played the cello. Twenty hours on the bus from Boston and the cello on the seat beside him. He paid for the extra ticket so the instrument wouldn't get lonely.

He was a smoker too, but not like you or I smoke. He exhaled, and then inhaled. He used to buy two packs at once, some Luckies and some Kamels with a K and take them all out and mix them up and put them back then. So you never knew what you would get. When he moved to the Spanish section of Chicago he learned German. He hated origami, but could do a thousand paper cranes in the time it took the grass to grow. He was the one who pointed out that magic today is really just public survival, like freezing yourself in a block of ice in Times Square and emerging many days later, frostbitten and barely breathing, but alive nonetheless. Once, he showed up to work as a bike messenger wearing a tuxedo. But he always wore his helmet. He knew chess and checkers, could say mate like he meant it.

He used to watch the grass grow.

I guess if you were once a genius you are always a genius. And if you were once in Chicago you probably still are. And wouldn't that be just like him to disappear for years then show up in the phone book instead of my subway car.

AMY L. CLARK

What I Really Meant Was That I Loved You

said these things to you, I said: I think only people who have never been arrested have sex with handcuffs on (but if you remember, that was when we were watching that movie and it was funny because of the other time, at the anti-war protest, when we got arrested together), and afterwards I said I didn't want to tell you what my position on Palestine is (as it turned out, of course, I had one too many drinks and I did talk about Palestine, and unexpectedly we agreed on a two-state solution), once, in the middle of the night, I asked, are you going to die? (apropos of universal health care, you had told me you have a heart condition and I wanted to know if it was a metaphor), and later I also said to you: so it's war now, is it? (but that was only because *The Herald* ran that headline IT'S WAR! many months after the war had been declared and a couple months after the president said it was over), and I said that the only way to subvert the militant patriarchal hierarchy was to fundamentally change the structure and nature of organized society by allowing anyone on the bottom to be on the top (it was probably the wrong time), but after all that I asked you if, really, you thought that, you know, considering, the ends could ever justify the means, like those suicide bombers exploding their desperate rapture all over public markets; and the thing is, you never answer me about the end.

DAVID SHUMATE

The Polka-Dot Shirt

The soldier returns to the city, dusty and alone. Nothing is as he remembers it. Buildings have vanished. Streets have been rolled up and carted away. Even his favorite whores are pregnant and married in the suburbs. He rents a room in a fancy hotel. He takes a long shower and while his scalp is still warm he shaves his head. He opens his suitcase and is surprised to find he has picked up someone else's luggage at the station by mistake. He unfolds a Hawaiian shirt and tries it on. Some khaki pants. A pair of loafers. He studies his reflection in the mirror and thinks he has seen this man before. Perhaps in a news report. Someone accused of swindling the elderly. Or an artist obsessed with flamingos. He takes the elevator to the hotel lobby and orders a drink at the bar. A woman regards him from a nearby table and smiles. Soon he is sitting with her, inventing a life as he goes along. After a few drinks she leans over and whispers something in his ear. He follows her up to her room and there they make love in the way she prefers. But the whole time he is distracted, wondering what will happen when he returns to his room and tries on the pants with the orange and yellow stripes. And the polka-dot shirt.

DAVID SHUMATE

Accordion Lessons

While others drank vodka and spread their legs for boys, the girl next door played polkas on her accordion all the years of her youth. Nothing about her family suggested this exotic instrument fit into their lives. They were not from Sicily or Guanajuato. They were not possessed of an irrational zest for life. When the daughter reached puberty, her parents doubled her practice time and her music echoed through the midnight neighborhood as if set loose from a painting by Chagall. Her mother had watched the virgins of Lawrence Welk and knew that as long as the girl played, she was safe from all seduction. Let the others chase boys. Let the others drink vodka. She took comfort in knowing that not even the Kama Sutra, the ancient scriptures of erotica, imagines a sex act involving an accordion and two consenting adults.

GAY DEGANI

Abbreviated Glossary

Want: I slide my naked leg between his thighs. Dev is trying a case tomorrow. He's tired, but he owes me his touch, and I know exactly how to use my tongue.

Pact: His lips disappear between his teeth when I break the news. He says he's not ready—no diapers for him—but I know he is. I'll do the hard part. I promise.

Hope: My fingers knead the curve of my belly. Dev slips an arm around my waist and grins at his boss. Proud papa.

Thrill: Dev can't keep his hands off me, calls me "sexy mama," but when he's not around, I fret. Eight months along and my bump so small.

Rift: Skull bones don't always fuse together, the doctor tells me. I call Dev, but he's in court, won't request a recess, even when I beg. The hard part, I see, will be losing both.

JAMES CLAFFEY

Kingmaker

The surgeon was off at golf, sweetly swinging his fairway wood. He shanked into the sand trap because of the phone's vibration. The text message outlined an accident involving a kidney and a sharp tool.

His patient was already prepped for theater, marked for the knife—not that the wound could be missed—a jagged red weal in his lower back. Poor bastard would be running on one engine for the rest of his life after the operation. He couldn't recall the nurse's name, or how he'd transgressed, but he did know she was from Tannourine El Faouqa. The Lebanon. His homeland.

He thought of his own people and their exile, driven across the planet by red-sanded winds and the whim of dictators. He cut the incision in a familiar shape, and only when the anesthesiologist coughed did he recognize he had serrated the borders of his homeland into the man's flesh. An obvious shape; close to a deer running at full pelt. Beads of sweat ran down his brow as he extended the incision to cover his error. This man would have quite the souvenir of his accident.

Energy depleted, he passed instrument after shiny steel instrument to the nurse, not the same woman he'd insulted, so he hazarded a look into her bright green eyes. He couldn't tell if she was attractive, or not, because of the mask hiding her mouth and nose, but he had created kingdoms, this man. He had created kingdoms.

PIA Z. EHRHARDT

Brides

The realtor brought me to see a light yellow cottage near the Tammany Trace. I was looking for my sister. "This neighborhood's safe for a woman alone," he said.

"She's engaged," I said. This had been true and I kept it that way.

"Does she need a big yard?" he said.

"No dog."

"A modern kitchen?"

"Small appetite."

"Garage?"

My ex-husband Ronnie rode a motorcycle with a seat fringed like a saddle that leaned my sister back, pelvis smiling up at him, hands on her thighs like arms on a chair. She'd never tired of the long rides to nowhere with our restless father. "Roll down your window," she'd tell me. The wind whipped her long hair at my face. "Tie it back," I'd tell her.

The realtor stood in the driveway. "This crape myrtle tree," he said, pointing over his head, "it stains carpet. There's room to put in a carport. For when it rains."

"She doesn't drive," I said.

The front door was beveled glass and unlocked. A pecan-sized cockroach skated across the hall. "Outside kind," the realtor said.

On his way to fuck my sister, Ronnie tried to beat the train at the crossing but his bike lost traction on the rails, slid him under a repair truck patient behind the wooden arm. I drove across Lake Pontchartrain to her place in New Orleans, took her in my arms. She wet my shirt with fresh tears. Mine stayed put imagining he'd long been dead to me.

"What will I do now?" she cried. "Move on my side," I said.

We were the before and after.

PEDRO PONCE

The Illustrated Woman

This was during better times. She called with her itinerary, reciting airline and gate numbers, her voice edged with hunger. I vacuumed, scrubbed, and laundered, shopped for two at the grocery store.

I waited at the gate, bouquet in hand. Next to me, a man was listening to the radio. The volume on his headphones was so loud, I could hear Liz Phair comparing a lover to the explosion of a dying star.

She surprised me from behind and pressed her lips to my ear. We collected her bags and left the terminal. I splurged for a cab. While the driver cursed between lane changes, I could feel the rush of the chassis through her clenched thighs.

We were barely through the door when she led me to the bedroom. We fell together, a tangle of hair and tongues. The front of her jeans gave way to my fingers. She lifted her hips and slid them down. An unfamiliar mark appeared just above her hip bone.

What is that? I asked.

She smiled and gathered the hem of her sweater up with both hands. It's Chinese, she said. Do you like it?

I leaned closer. It was a symbol I recognized from bumper stickers and New Age bookstores. Two tailless fish—one black, one white—curled next to each other to form a circle.

I thought you hated needles.

I hate getting shots, she said. I've always wanted a tattoo.

She was drawn to its simplicity, centuries of wisdom inscribed on her skin. Two sides in opposition yet necessary to make a whole, discrete yet inseparable.

It made me think of you, she said. Besides, I didn't like any of the other designs. Can you imagine me with a sunflower on my ass?

What about my name? I said.

She wrestled me to the mattress, laughing. Silly, she said.

Later, I couldn't sleep. I got out of bed and sat by the window, watching her. Her legs kicked free of the sheets. With every breath, the shapes inked on her skin rose and fell, two halves and the indelible border between.

PEDRO PONCE

One of Everything

I decided to celebrate my freedom. It was nowhere near the Fourth of July. I made a table out of a splintery plank and stacked milk crates. Over this, I draped a paint-splattered tarp.

I went through my kitchen and took out plates, cups, forks, knives, spoons. I took the salt shaker, left the pepper shaker. I came upon two saucepans humping lovelessly in the dish rack. Simplify, I said, separating them. I kept one of everything. The rest I took outside.

My selection was limited and customers were few. A neighbor from next door turned the full salt shaker suspiciously in one hand. A quarter, I said. No charge for the salt. She set the shaker down and left for a sale down the street.

By afternoon, I had still sold nothing. Two women approached to inspect my table. The prettier of the two wore a wedding band and smelled like sunscreen and the ocean. She ran a bronzed finger along the flowered rim of a bowl.

Are you moving? she asked.

I told her no, I was simplifying. I was here to stay.

She considered some silverware and a stack of plates but a loud honk drew her away. A rental truck pulled up to the house across from mine. She leaned into the driver's window. A light breeze rippled the back of her skirt.

It was close to dark when I went inside. I taped a sign to my table that said FREE in big block letters.

ELIZABETH ELLEN

Panama City by Daylight

My daughter was in the tub. This was Tuesday: bath day. I had a far off look on my face. My body was in the bathroom, kneeled, before her. My mind was somewhere else: Memphis, maybe, or Moscow. "You're falling out of love with him, aren't you?" she asked. And by him she of course meant you. "No," I said. "There are ebbs and flows in relationships. This is a time of ebb. That's all." "You're not a very good girlfriend," she said, before submerging herself under water. She was practicing holding her breath. I was supposed to be counting the seconds.

You asked me the same question last week. You said, "You seem distant." Which was your version of "You don't love me as much anymore, do you?"

I was in Hattiesburg then but I didn't admit so.

"No," I said. "I'm right here."

I offered you a weak smile and dove into the pool. I floated to the bottom and made a tidy home on the floor. I turned on my side like I do in bed with you. I closed my eyes, slowed my breathing. I can stay down here a long time, I thought. I was halfway to Tallahassee already; I planned on making Panama City by daylight.

ELIZABETH ELLEN

8 × 10

In an unfamiliar room you disrobe, removing only bra/no panties, as previously discussed, as heretofore agreed to. An hour ago you sent your husband into the corner 7-11 for diapers and he returned with a porcelain rabbit and pack of chewing gum. His character has recently come into question. His entire act is up for review. You feed his child with a breast he begrudgingly shares while on the other side of the wall he entertains an unsuspecting audience with his one-man show. "I'm going to shoot that kid," he says, making a gun of his thumb and forefinger and pointing it at the right temple of the man in the mirror. "I used to snort cocaine off a model's ass. Those days are over," he continues, arms in the air, pausing for dramatic effect.

In the 8×10 broom closet where they store him he will refuse to open his mouth. No more soliloquies, the doctor will tell you with a smile and a handshake, as though bad theatre were ample enough reason for the removal of a tongue. Left alone with your husband you stare at him through the glass above the door and he stares back at you, his eyes static, his mouth a single straight line:_____. You study him, remembering how it feels to stand before the ocelot at the zoo: like unmitigated self-pity, like you could move the bars with your eyes if only he'd lift a paw to help.

Watch now the baby grow fat. Watch her gorge herself on your milk, forgetting what it means to share. Read to her from her book of ABCs. "O" is for ocelot, you say, remembering that the average life span of an ocelot is 10–13 years in the wild, 20 in captivity.

DINTY W. MOORE

Rumford

Given how Uncle Skitch drank, no one in the family wanted to believe him when he insisted that Rumford could speak.

No one wanted Skitch to drive, either, but he did.

In the mornings, still stung from the four or five tumblers of whiskey he downed at the kitchen table the night before while shouting at the voices on his radio, Skitch would stumble out his front door, fumble into his massive, gray 1962 Buick—"the battleship"—and jerk-stop, jerk-stop, jerk-stop the damn car all the way to the end of the block before realizing his emergency brake was still engaged. He did this repeatedly, refusing to learn. The noise horrified everyone.

But old Skitch jerk-stopped his battleship to its final mooring spot when the railroad finally let him go. Skitch used to ride in the back of the train, watching out for equipment failure. After he lost the job, he just drank around the clock, and never drove anywhere.

The neighbors were more relieved than annoyed to see that old Buick rotting out front.

Skitch still bragged about Rumford, though.

If you called Skitch at home, the dog would answer the phone. Or that is what Skitch said, anyway. Most of us thought it was his wife, Ethel. She had a deep voice from all those years of chain-smoking unfiltered Pall Malls. She loved a good practical joke.

Three years later, Skitch and Ethel vanished. The Buick disappeared from the curb. Mail piled up. The phone wasn't answered. My father finally broke into the house to find no one at home, no note, but all the clothes missing.

Police quizzed the only witness.

Rumford didn't say a thing.

MICHELLE ELVY

Triptych

The triptych, left: a whaling boat, riding high on rough seas. The tail of the whale is wrapped in ropes, thrashing; the boat is a bobbing wooden toy. The curator points—*Class, listen*—and speaks of form and shading. Girls squirm and boys move in close. John shuffles forward and is pressed behind Marianne. He worries he smells of sweat. Beth, to Marianne's right, turns and glares. Beth is always at Marianne's side. They have matching sweaters. John is wedged in, trapped behind the girls. His arm brushes against Marianne's. Beth takes Marianne's hand: a barricade of laced fingers.

The triptych, right: whale beaten and beached, men standing triumphantly atop his back; meat has been sliced from the creature's body and laid out on the beach. John lowers his head and tries to move right, away from such close proximity to honey-scented hair, but now he is forced forward, between Beth and Marianne. The front of his trousers brush against their still clasped hands. Beth shoots him a mean look, cuts right through him.

The triptych, middle (the largest image): the boat alongside the great creature, the first harpoon stuck in firm, the harpoonist perched with second harpoon raised. Ready for the kill. The crewmen row to keep steady. The boat rides on frothy waves. A grotesque and dizzying moment. John's skin stings at the sight of the harpoon. The curator's rising voice—*Class, look!*—chills his spine. John is sweating profusely now, squished between Marianne's prickly sweater and Beth's cruel gaze. The curator's voice stabs into his head. He closes his eyes and rides the waves.

MICHELLE ELVY

Antarctica

The man finds the boy in a drainpipe and when he asks him *what are you doing in there?* the boy looks at him as if he should already know and says *I'm looking for Antarctica.* Later at home, the man's wife catches him staring at the tiny specks of dust spiralling in the late-afternoon sun and when she asks *What are you thinking?* for about the millionth time he hates her but he also knows he'd hate it even more if she stopped asking so he shrugs and says *I'm thinking about Antarctica.*

He goes back the next day and the boy is gone. He waits for him because he knows there's something they needed to say but forgot. The sky is heavy metallic: the hour before snowfall. He pulls his collar tight and heads home and when he gets there his wife's standing naked in the kitchen. It has started to snow and the only color in the room is the orange of her fingernails. The snow falls and they can't get warm, no matter how hard they make love. Later he's staring again and his wife says *Antarctica?* but how could she know he's more than a million miles away with the boy in the drainpipe.

He returns to the drainpipe and crouches down on his hands and knees. His shoulders barely fit but he wedges himself in. He is about to turn and crawl down the pipe, all the way to a new continent, when a stranger walks by and sees him and when he asks *what are you doing in there?* the man looks at the stranger as if he should already know.

DAMIAN DRESSICK

Four Hard Facts About Water

1. Mixed with Dewar's White Label whiskey and served in a highball glass with shaved ice, it will cost nearly eleven dollars, on average, in most bars within two blocks of New York City's Houston Street.

2. Many Christians believe a thorough dousing in concert with a contrite heart represents a first, but critically important, step on the road to the development and maintenance of a personal relationship with Jesus Christ.

3. Breaststroke, backstroke, butterfly, Australian crawl, take your pick—as Pennsylvania's Junior State Champion 1994, you go through it like a fish.

4. After your two-year-old daughter trips and falls unseen into the neighbor's in-ground pool while you are in their summer house trying to find steak sauce, your involvement with Fact One can consume your life, costing you your spouse and job and nearly, if not quite all, your self-esteem. Fact Two will be rendered utterly powerless in the face of this tragedy and Fact Three will come to be the way you define irony—when slurring to strangers who have already asked you once to please leave them alone as closing time approaches at O'Flanagan's, always a little quicker than you'd like.

KATHY FISH

The Possibility of Bears

We'd been drinking wine and eating leftover wedding cake on the deck. I'd chosen rainbow colored frosting. It was supposed to taste like strawberries.

"I shouldn't be drinking," I said.

"Then stop."

We were staying in a cabin in a national forest. The first thing we saw as we lugged our suitcases from the car were claw marks on the door. I asked if they were real. He said he suspected so.

Behind the cabin was a cornfield, which seemed out of place. I had wanted to go to Switzerland, but this place was okay. Cheaper.

He started cleaning up.

I said, "Well, look at that view."

He wetted his finger and opened a garbage bag.

"Gosh, you're so fastidious," I said, but it came out wrong, sounded more like facetious. I read the label on the wine. A peppery finish, it said.

He reminded me about the possibility of bears.

I watched him sweep, moving in and out of the shadows. I tried to think if we'd been to any movies lately. There was an old style movie house five miles down the road in the little town, showing The Three Stooges.

"We could try to find Stephen King's vacation house," I said.

He continued to sweep.

"I think you can stop now," I said.

I pointed out the hot tub, but his head was turned to some noise in the woods. He said, "I'm not exactly a Boy Scout."

"Neither am I."

Like wine, the hot tub was probably not good for me either.

He sat down. I toed off my slippers, forked cake into his mouth.

"Eat this," I said. "Eat every last bite." And he chewed and stared. When we were first living together, we used to do this. Feed each other. Lick things off each other's bodies. After the ceremony he'd found some emails. I said they were old. But they weren't old enough. And now here we were. Married.

"Wait. I hear it now."

"That's the sound of a bear protecting its baby."

I heard it again. Closer.

"Cub," I said.

KATHY FISH

Akimbo

We're painting the nursery in the nude. Slapping eggshell over walls the color of a baby's tongue. We've been at it awhile. The pink keeps bleeding through. We're not using drop cloths because the carpet's getting ripped up anyway—this sort of sculpted wall-to-wall that reminds me of my grandmother's house and smells like cigarettes and corn. So we're manic about it, spattering ourselves, our glasses, our hair and forearms, our privates. You paint a heart on your chest. I smear a swath across my forehead. A Flock of Seagulls song plays on the radio. There's a tremor and it makes us stop. Now a jolt and you go, *Whoa Nellie*. The windowglass trembles. Bits of plaster copter to the floor. Paint sloshes out of the can. You're trying to reach me and all I can think of is the electric football game me and my brothers had when we were kids and how we'd work forever setting up our offensive and defensive lines and when we'd finally flip the switch, all the little plastic players just stood in one place and vibrated impotently. This is you now, beautiful and vibrating, your arms akimbo, looking like all you want is to break free, achieve forward momentum, catch me, before the world splits apart.

ROBERT VAUGHAN

What's Left Unsaid

He turned the car off, exhausted. The drive had seemed endless, hours elongated like taffy. He stretched his arms behind his head, challenged his burning eyes to stay open. In the distance, he could see the wisp rising from their sugarhouse chimney. He figured she'd be up already. A crack of dawn slipped through pillowed clouds, more dark than light. He loped toward the house, opened the kitchen door, set his bags down.

As he crossed the pasture, Serena whinnied inside the barn. She always sensed when he was close. He paused under a maple, looked down at his calfskin Tony Lamas. Wondered how he might explain blowing all their retirement savings in Vegas. Maybe he could work more overtime, save up again. Then he wouldn't have to tell her.

ROBERT VAUGHAN

Time for Dessert

The couple sits on their front porch every summer night. Although the view remains the same, they never tire of it. The steady river birches in the side yard. A martin's house across the road. Darting swallows chatter, catching multitudes of bugs.

He says, "Warmer this evening." Sucks down the last bit of his third Manhattan, nibbles the cherry.

She nods, pulls the sleeves down on her cashmere sweater. Can't seem to ever get warm enough. She points. "Look at how huge that ship is."

"They usually don't let barges like that on the St. Lawrence."

It's the main reason they moved to such a remote location. He loves water, boats, and all the activities associated with them. That, and he'd also burned through most of their friends before retirement age. One too many drunken spats. They sit and watch boats motor by. A bee buzzes on the roses near the screened door.

"Are you ready for dessert?" she asks. "Fresh peach pie."

"Yup."

She ambles inside and he stares at her rocker's motion, hypnotized. He sets it to an old favorite melody, Ella's "Let's Call the Whole Thing Off." From the kitchen he hears the familiar sound of plates clinking, the microwave beeps. He sees a fancy motorboat toting a teenaged skier. His mouth waters.

Tomorrow, he thinks, I'm going to get up early and go fishing.

All by myself.

MELISSA FRATERRIGO

Momma's Boy

Joseph flung open the back door of the two-bedroom rental home and sprinted into the bathroom while Carlotta paid bills at the table, the help-wanted ads in a stack at her left, breakfast dishes still soaking in the sink. "Joey? What do you have?"

She shut the door. The fan on top of the refrigerator blew a hot gust on her face. Yesterday it was a kitten. Three days ago he brought home a gray rabbit from a girl two blocks over. If they lived closer to her brothers, Carlotta wouldn't worry about Joey, but Detroit was a six-hour ride by train and with her salary at Sunshine Dental, they wouldn't be making any trips until Christmas. "Joseph Michael Vespi, I'm talking to you."

He unlocked the door and crept into the kitchen. Mud speckled his glasses; his dark bangs slumped against his forehead. Joseph held out his cupped palms and inside was a green and yellow-shelled thing. "It's a turtle, mom. He was sitting near the train tracks. I saved him."

"Joey." Tugging on his wrist, she led him outside. Squinting into the light, Carlotta placed the turtle on the sidewalk; it remained motionless. "Now hit him. You're a boy." Joey trembled. "No crying, hit him." He bent down and tapped its shell with two fingers. Snot dribbled from the end of his nose. Carlotta drew her hand into a fist and pounded its shell. "You're a boy. A boy." She smacked it again and something popped and the turtle flattened. Suddenly her breath snapped and jerked out of her lungs; she was tossed backwards, the pavement burning her skin. Joey stood on top of her, his shoes making two muddy blobs on her blouse. She peered up at him. "Good," she said. "That's good."

MICHAEL MARTONE

Miners

Going east, I cross the Ohio by a bridge that empties on the west side smack into a mountain face tunneled through to Wheeling. Set back from the highway on the old roadbeds are the miners' houses. Mountains are at their back door. The highway cuts through the mountains, and on the sheer faces of the cliffs on both sides, I see where they've bored and set the charges like a pencil split in two and the lead removed.

I think about the products of coal. The stockings you wear. The records you play. The aspirin you take. The pencil you write with. These are mine. What would we do without all this carbon?

As I move, the face of the land is changing. I am going east so I can write to you.

The hillsides are quarries mining men. The men are going home where they will discover that all the waters in Shakespeare will not make them clean. This life has gotten under their skins. They make love in smudges.

I am going further east where men are inside of things, where they own things inside and out.

I am writing this with a pencil painted yellow and printed with a silhouette of a woman with no arms.

I wish I were a miner so that when you turned your back to me and the face of the land changed, before I would go back underground, I would reach out and write with my black finger some graphite text on the places you could not reach.

"You," it would say, "are mine."

MICHAEL MARTONE

Dan Quayle Thinking: On Snipe Hunting

They told me to wait, so I wait. They gave me a burlap sack and pushed me out of the car into the ditch next to a field. I watched the taillights disappear. They told me they would drive the snipes my way. "Wait here." And I do.

Stars are in the sky. I'm in a mint field. The branches of the low bushes brush against my legs, releasing the reeking smell.

I think, suddenly, they are not coming back. Back home, they are waiting for me to figure out they are not coming back. They are thinking of this moment, the one happening now, when I think this thought, that they are not coming back, and then come home on my own.

But, I think, I'll wait. While waiting, I'll think of them waiting for me to return home with the empty burlap sack. They'll think that I haven't thought, yet, that I was left here in the mint field, that I am waiting for them to drive the snipes my way. I'll let them think that.

In the morning, I'll be here, waiting. They will come back looking for me. Dew will have collected on the mint bushes. The stars will be there but will be invisible. And I won't have thought that thought yet, the one they wanted me to think.

The imaginary quarry is still real and still being driven my way.

PAUL BECKMAN

Brother Speak

My brother and I speak. He says, "Hey." I say, "Hey" back and he gives me a light punch in the shoulder. I fake a punch to his gut and say, "Hey."

He waves me away and I fake going after him, he turns and fakes a kick to my groin. I say, "Whoa" and turn. He laughs and fakes another and I say, "I said whoa" and he laughs again and punches me in my bicep with a punch that's not a love tap as much as a warning tap.

Our wives come and get us for dinner. I ask him to pass me a dinner roll and he says, "Hey" and tosses one across the table. The family laughs and he asks for the salt and I grab for the salt planning to send it flying his way but my wife gets to it first and says, "Hey" and passes it civilly down his side of the table.

After dinner and before dessert we all go out and play touch football with a Nerf ball and when he touches me he says, "Hah" and touches me really hard.

I'm close to clocking him when the wives yell for us to come in and get coffee and dessert. We, my brother and I, sit around the table not talking but listening to the women and kids chatter nonstop.

He pushes back his chair and says, "Yo, gotta go," and his wife gathers up the kids and they walk out to the car and he taps me on the head and says, "Hey," and I knuckle punch his shoulder and say, "Bye" and he makes a move at me and I flinch and he laughs and says "Hey, hey—still a flincher," and off they go from their yearly visit.

TIFF HOLLAND

Hot Work

The transvestites like scarves although none of the women in the shop wear them, not anymore. The transvestites are slippers-in, after closing. They're incognito in the back room and emerge sweaty flowers. It is hot work, being beautiful, but they are willing to make the concessions, to pay cash so their wives cannot track their other lives. They try on the wigs gathering dust on the top shelves, the ones the beauty shop ladies spurn. It is just them and us although they would like nothing more than to mingle under the dryers, to nibble donuts and discuss the *Enquirer*. My mother applies their makeup. I feign sleep in the shampoo chair, sneaking a peek at the finished products: unwinged angels with five o'clock shadows, tottering in circles between the dryers and the styling chairs, trying in that small space to learn how to fly.

JEFF LANDON

Flying

Say we met. Say we met in Virginia and it was snowing in the mountains, and we were standing at the top of a steep hill with a toboggan in my hands, a blue toboggan, and say we were laughing, a little high from your brother's pot, holding on to each other with mittened hands. We could huddle around a tiny bonfire with hot chocolate in one thermos and hot buttered rum in the other, and puff the night air with our words and your cigarette smoke. We would be the tallest people on the top of the hill, the grownups, and behind us, over an iced ridge of pine trees, a Chevron sign would glow neon red and blue, and you'd shiver and take off your stocking cap to shake out the ice from your hair. We would face each other on the blue toboggan, side by side, and listen to the way a small town feels after the first real snow in years. And let's say we're laughing and new to each other—let's forget about all the years and the quiet distance.

Our coats crinkle when we move, and right before takeoff you loop your arms around me and we're flying, flying down a hill on a blue toboggan. Stars pour down on pine trees and snow, and I can feel your smile on my neck, a crooked smile, and we slide down that hill and near the end of our ride we kiss each other hard, kiss like teenagers in someone's dark basement, with our bodies pressed together, and we look like one large person, a lumpy one, flying down a hill that is steeper than any hill we ever imagined, back then.

JOSH RUSSELL

Our Boys

Our boys are born two years apart, and we dress our second son in his brother's hand-me-downs. As children, their faces and haircuts are so alike, we later can't figure out in snapshots which one's which unless they both appear, so we halve the stack of photographs in which they're alone, make two albums, label the first with the firstborn's name, the second with the second's. Our boys don't notice. They bring home girlfriends, boyfriends, wives, offspring. Nobody figures it out. First the secret's delightful—we've tricked our clever kids!—then troubling. We thought we'd made our boys carefully, raised two individuals. We thought we were exhausted because we'd loved each with unique fervor. How can we now not recognize their differences? We study missing teeth, the Snoopy T-shirt's faded collar, the weight of the cat in their laps. When the phone rings in the middle of the night, we worry it's one of our boys, and if we answer and he greets us, we won't know to whom we're speaking.

JOSH RUSSELL

Black Cat

Remember prom, boutonniere pressed flat as if it'd been preserved in a book. Remember heat radiating through rented pants, through creaking tulle skirts, more than the heat of first sex. Remember blood on the sheet, the twitch of pleasure that shook her. Remember college, Saturday nights becoming Sunday mornings, coffee and the *Post* in bed, comics and front page kicked to the floor, sliding and crashing like water. Remember the breakup. Remember hours of pool with Physics major sharps who could not lose. Remember running into her at Sibbie's party senior year. Remember being naked in the Honda in the parking lot, rain like code on the roof, windows fogging, then glowing as dawn broke. Remember the Christmas tree blown into the middle of the street in which the black cat played. Remember laughing at her while she stood at the second story window clad only in a blanket conversing in Spanish with Mormons, too polite to ignore the bell. Remember the months during which the only reasons you wanted to see each other were to fuck and have your papers proofread. Remember driving away to Baton Rouge, long lists of vows trailing. Remember the second breakup. Remember sadness and loneliness like possessions taking up space in the room. Remember your birthday falling on Thanksgiving, the trip north, how she gave herself like a gift. Remember Christmas. Remember the night she begged to be taken back and you, standing barefoot on the tiny rusted landing, looking at the alley's luminous shell gravel and listening to her voice being pulled thin by a thousand miles of fiber optics, sure that prospects for love were numerous in that weird city, said no.

CHRISTOPHER MERKNER

Children at the Bar

They aren't at all slow or simple. They totally get reproach. The man shares a steady, mannered gaze with his wife before turning to say, Dude, *you're in a bar. A bar.* You brought your children *to a bar.* It's accurate. My wife says, Hear this, but it's accurate. We are in a bar with the kids. The burritos are amazing. If you want burritos like this, you field words like theirs. Then, again. And the vulgar couple isn't satisfied: they come over and pull in. They float a few more sailors, directly to our faces. I avert, look at our kids. They are getting the words and their parents being named by these words. The vulgar lady moves swiftly, slips her mouth over my wife's; then the dude has his mouth on mine. I don't know what the vulgar lady is doing to my wife, but he is very rough on the face. He is blowing some pretty dark shit in there. It's interesting. The kids are nonplussed: the burritos are really just *really* good here. My wife's suddenly a head on the table. I fight, a weak jog of the neck, maybe two, but ultimately I let him keep blowing because I'm still strangely certain I have more space inside than he possibly could, and I am willing to take it to see this play out, and frankly it feels like it's just what I need these kids to see.

TARA LASKOWSKI

We're Gonna Be Here Awhile

And it snowed. And it blackened. And when I called Leslie from the county jail I told her I did it to get out of the storm. And she sighed, that's all, and before she could say something I couldn't hear I hung up. The officer helped me bandage up my arm. He asked me if it was worth it. Outside someone's tires were spitting as they tried to pull out of their parallel space. The officer told me he used to live in Key West, but he couldn't stand the humidity or the key lime everything. He had a mustache you could lose pea soup in, and a filthy way of rubbing his nose with his fingers. The jewelry storeowner was coming to give a statement, and while we waited we listened to the hum of the generator and watched the receptionist lose at FreeCell. Behind the officer's head on the bulletin board there was a picture of a cat holding a bottle of Sam Adams in its paws and a crooked photocopy of the poem "Footprints." The jewelry storeowner called, said he couldn't get out of his driveway. I tried to remember why any of it was a good idea. The officer put his hands behind his head, leaned back in his squeaky chair and looked at me in that way that waiters do when you walk in on Christmas Day or New Year's Eve, a resigned distaste for what has led to this particular moment.

TARA LASKOWSKI

Dendrochronology

It was 10th grade, the year of Hurricane Isaac, which mowed down the mighty oak in the teachers' parking lot, snapped it like a cinnamon stick and prompted Mr. Luckanza to teach us about dendrochronology, counting the tree's rings. Grown-ups wanted to turn everything into a lesson.

It was the year the football team had a shot, and they introduced cheese fries into the cafeteria. We had to take English 10 and read dog-eared copies of "How Green Was My Valley?" which everyone kept calling "How Long Is My Valley?" The economy tanked and my mom took a second shift at the late-night diner. We all turned 16 and some of us got parties. The biggest one was Shannon Richardson's, talked about for months because someone vomited all over her parents' white suede sofa and she posted flyers on certain lockers looking for a confession.

It was the year people started losing their virginity, whether on purpose or not. Then, right before Christmas break, they found Mr. Luckanza in his car with a pistol in his lap and a shattered windshield stained red the color of those poisonous berries our parents always warned us not to eat. In the spring, a group of men came in overalls to finally take the oak away, chain-sawing it in pieces and tossing the hunks over the side of their pick-up. Even after they drove away I could still imagine rolling my fingers along the tree's insides, the roughness of the bark and the tenderness of the inside, some rings small, some larger, some stained dark and hardened like a cancer, almost like it knew what was coming but couldn't tell anyone until it was too late.

MICHAEL CZYZNIEJEWSKI

Intrigued by Reincarnation,
Skip Dillard Embraces Buddhism

When you have a next life, there's no such thing as a one-on-one. The concept of not getting a second chance after failing on the first is so Western, it's no wonder we're always at war. Imagine a world where redemption is only a step off the roof away. Tripping in front of a bus would do it, too, and so would two bottles of Tylenol. A hungry bear in the woods. A lucky bolt of lightning. Colon cancer. No matter what you were guilty of, or innocent, you could start over any time you wanted. Sure, a margin of error exists. You could come back as an infectious microbe. A sickly leopard. The maggot born in the trash can behind some Chinese take-out joint. But you might get lucky, too, end up rich, a beautiful actress, married to a handsome athlete, always on the news for her charitable tendencies. You could be a famous doctor. An inventor. The first man to do something no one's ever done before, like walk on Mars or travel back in time. You could be the lap dog to that same beautiful actress, traveling in her purse, your picture in a thousand magazines, a kiss on the nose for every flash of the camera. Even better, you could be nobody. You could go about your business, live your life. Minor victories would go unnoticed, as would major defeats. Even if anyone turned around to look, it wouldn't matter. Either you wouldn't care, or you'd move on again, the next roll of the dice. If you kept shooting, sooner or later, you'd get better at it, always get something good. Like you were money in the bank.

MICHAEL CZYZNIEJEWSKI

Eating William Wells' Stout Heart, Fort Dearborn, 1812

n your hand, it feels like it's still beating. The hardest part isn't the kill, or the careful removal with a dull knife. It's shaking the notion that you're about to consume something alive, something whole, that it might scream out in horror when you break the skin with your teeth. Picture holding a small animal between your thumbs and pointers—a squirrel, a bat, a pike—then biting down into its shoulder. It is warm, full of blood, and trying its best to slip free, to claw you to shreds. The only thing that makes you go through with it is your audience, everyone waiting for their turn, wanting their share of bravery, strength, and verisimilitude. Deep down, you know they're thinking the same thing you are, that there are better paths to self-improvement. But first in line is an honor; you get the best piece, the most potent hunk. Your tribesmen aren't the only ones watching, either. There are the others, behind the wall, witnessing why they call you savage firsthand. It becomes a pissing match at that point—who can be more turned off by what you've done, by what you're about to do. You start to wonder if this is the only way to work out your differences, and then, as your hand drips red, you swear you feel another pulse. In the end, you know you'll go through with it. That you have no choice. Otherwise, it would be an awful waste.

LEN KUNTZ

Lens

If you look close, you can see me in her photo—I am the elongated stain in the northeast section of her mirrored sunglass frame. It's our anniversary and I should be smiling but she is—after a summer of murder, she's the one smiling—and since I've never seen her offer an expression like this before I'm mostly stumped, car-struck and nervous, but you'd never know because the lens blocks my face, and anyway, as I said, I'm simply a spot on the glass, a smudge, a smear, a white-crusted bird dropping.

Yesterday she stuffed the roses I bought down the disposal. I came back in to retrieve my forgotten wallet and found her feeding limbs into the manic metal mouth. A motor tore up the stems and stamens, the thorns and chlorophyll. She stood over the sink watching. She ran water. She might have been weeping, I'm not sure, but I do know for a fact that she was laughing.

She couldn't see me, didn't realize I was there, but I had a feeling we were both wondering over the same thing, the ease of destruction, how simple it is to kill a living thing, unborn child or store-bought bouquet.

LEN KUNTZ

The Hard Dance

Before she leaves for the weekend, my daughter asks me if I'll teach her how to slow dance.

When she was young she took hip-hop classes, so chubby with all the other blades. The following year, chubby gave way to fat. She wore sweats and only continued for my wife's sake, for mine. In those outfits the spandex looked like a mudslide and I found myself looking away at the other girls who were more fit and prettier, blonder, with clean teeth.

When I put my hands on her hips now, she winces.

I yell, "Damn it!"

She says it's okay, it's just a few small bruises, it's not what I think, Russell wasn't even around when it happened, he was in Chicago, he was, he was.

I pull her close. Her pulse throbs through her wrist. He'll be holding her like this, I think.

In the ceiling I see a new crack, a gray streak of crooked lightning from where the house has settled. Then I notice others a few feet away. Those'll need to be fixed, I tell myself.

When we put the sign in the yard my daughter went berserk, tossed the toaster through the kitchen window. "I know why you're doing this!" she screamed. "You two can go ahead and move if you want, but I'm staying."

Now we sway, our shoe tips brushing. We cut odd concentric paths round and round right there in the living room where I watched her take her first step.

She squeezes my hand. She leans in and tells me she loves him. She says he makes her happy.

DEBRA MARQUART

Dylan's Lost Years

Somewhere between Hibbing and New York, the red rust streets of the Iron Range and the shipping yards of the Atlantic, somewhere between Zimmerman and Dylan was a pit stop in Fargo, a superman-in-the-phone-booth interlude, recalled by no one but the Danforth Brothers, who hired the young musician, fresh in town with his beat-up six string and his small town twang, to play shake, rattle, and roll, to play good golly, along with Wayne on the keys and Dirk on the bass, two musical brothers whom you might still find playing the baby grand, happy hours at the southside Holiday Inn.

And if you slip the snifter a five, Wayne might talk between how high the moon, and embraceable you, about Dylan's lost years, about the Elvis sneer, the James Dean leather collar pulled tight around his neck, about the late night motorcycle rides, kicking over the city's garbage cans, and how they finally had to let him go, seeing how he was more trouble than he was worth, and with everyone in full agreement that the new boy just could not sing.

DEBRA MARQUART

This New Quiet

The day after the fire, all their equipment charred in a ditch and blown to ashes, the thin axle of the truck lying on its side like the burned-out frame of a dragonfly, they gathered in a living room on a circle of old couches. The players sat forward, their eyes studying the swirls in the worn carpet.

They who had the power to make so much noise sat in this new quiet. They did not speak of debt or creditors, nor did they speak of lost guitars—the blond Les Paul, and the mahogany Gibson double-neck that sang sweetly in its velvet case as it rolled down the highway.

They sat in silence, trying to find the new words the fire had left on their tongues. Outside traffic rushed by, the clatter of passing trains, the honk of angry horns, as the sun dialed its way around the room and disappeared.

In the half dark someone stood. It was the tall blond guitar player who rose, wobbly in his black boots. He stood in the center of the spiral, raised his thin hands to his face and blew out one long exhale. It hissed through the room like a wild balloon losing steam.

When all the wind was out of him, he gulped one deep breath, swung a long arm like a knockout punch through the sheer emptiness of air, and said, *Fuck*. It was only one word. It was inadequate for the moment. But it was a good place to start.

ROY KESEY

Calisthenics

There was a perfect rectangle and he walked outside, down the block, and now the restaurant. The restaurant girl, beautiful through the window. He did a jumping jack but she turned away.

Farther on a woman and she smacked him against a wall. The wall smelled terrific, cool and damp and cementy as he fell. He hit the ground, chipped a tooth, looked up at her huge against the sun.

A ride and some questions and painted bars for a while. Sweet sweet cement but his tooth hurt a lot. A guy offered him a thing and took him by the scruff of his neck. Then someone came for him. She said things and he nodded a lot. Most people were mostly right.

At home the person was still saying things and to make his tooth hurt less he imagined that it was an elephant. The restaurant girl, was she calling out to the cook? He hoped that she was and tomorrow he would find her and ask her.

Night. The television had things and he watched them. The restaurant girl would just now be getting home and still have grease on her hands, sweat on her face, he was sure of it. Time, time. The television things moved. She only wanted for him to be happy. He did a toe-touch, and then another.

ROY KESEY

Learning to Count in a Small Town

1

stands in his garden at dawn. On the trunk of his apricot tree is a swallowtail fanning its wings still wet with birth. *Ven,* he calls to his wife. *Ha nacido la mariposa.*

2

pushes her cart through the supermarket, around and around in the cool air. Her mouth is crusted with dirt. When she tires, she rests. She buys a bag of dog food, and the clerk knows she has no dog. He nods and hands her the receipt.

3

hasn't yet learned to swim. Her brother taunts her from the far side of the river. The light on the water hurts her eyes. She looks down at her feet and wishes they were smaller.

leans on the bathroom sink and stares at himself in the mirror. There is more yellow in his left eye than in his right. The phone rings. He goes on staring.

hammers on the podium, shouts about immigrants. In the park outside the auditorium, men are playing softball, swearing and spitting, and their wives pretend to watch.

leans back in her hammock and knows that the afternoon heat will never end. The stink of tarweed weights the air. Crows harry a red-tailed hawk through the sky.

just makes it to his mailbox. Inside is the water bill and a postcard from his granddaughter. *I hope you're okay,* she has written. *I hope everything is fine.*

never leaves her apartment. She rests on the floor, stares out the screen door at the dusk and her empty bird feeder.

sits up in bed and lights a cigarette. If she holds her breath she can hear the television in the next room.

has heart trouble. From his barstool he listens to conversations and has thoughts of football. He asks for one more drink and the barman says, *Sorry, bud. We're finished here. It's time to get you home.*

KATHLEEN McGOOKEY

Another Drowning, Miner Lake

A woman drowned last night in our lake, she was drowning but we didn't know: we saw flashing lights, a police car drove by our house. Drowning: the helicopter landed and all the cars backed out of the driveway. We heard on the police scanner it was a woman or a girl. Though her chance was slim, the sun set as usual, gorgeous and temporary despite the rain, a small sweet promise to our skin from the world. Promise of green, a gray dawn, a day that stretches long and without kisses or appointments. As much as we'd like to think we're elevated, we're not. We thought she was a little girl but it turned out she was older. We hadn't known her and still we swam, knew this about her, swam to the diving raft and someone's yard light shone white over us. No one can blame the lake; concentrate instead on saving yourself, myself, the self I have covered with wings, because today the lake is simple and gray and going through the motions, calm—flat as a plate, polite as any gilded mirror.

KYLE HEMMINGS

Supergirl

On TV seasons ago she played Supergirl. Now running along the slip of beach, performing her mile jog and panting, she slowed and collapsed before my sand castle. Her body was no longer a fiddle, but rather, a cello.

"It's what being out of work does to you," she said with that innocent air of the everyday tragic, that inarticulate murmur between words.

We turned and forked our hands into sand, piled clumps of wet sand onto the castle. We were still like kids, I thought.

Later, we rolled over and welcomed the sun into the plexus of our pale bodies.

"You still don't love me, do you, Supergirl?"

She turned one slow sleepy eye toward me.

"It'll be the way it always was. I'll be your mermaid and I'll fuck like one. But when it comes to love, this old Supergirl will fly away."

She closed her eyes and turned her head toward the sand.

"That season ended a long time ago," she said.

I reached for her breast under the white bathing suit. It felt like ice, or maybe an imitation ice sculpture of a breast, melting.

KYLE HEMMINGS

Father Dunne's School for Wayward Boys #1

There must have been a black-holed galaxy of eyes watching us, Father Dunne's special boys, who secretly wished to be crucified. We tucked our plastic rosaries into our back pockets, the same ones where we once kept rainbow-colored condoms. There were awkward confessions in the corner of a room that always made us shiver with long-suppressed intimacies. Our hearts would never again be open to visitors.

The proctor with early dementia sang at night through the only open window for miles. Something about stars on a string and how his mother did amazing needlepoint until her fingers went stiff. We told the star-crossed priests with traces of old acne that our mothers did tricks to save our bodies. Our pen knives were confiscated so we sharpened our pencils and used them for weapons.

A young girl wavering between celibacy and punk mother-lust despair came to visit us each night. In a dim light, she blushed pink.

She sowed our loins in different patterns with her brilliant coordination of tongue and complex fingering, then walked away, blending with morning sky. We became a wet dream. With magic marker, we drew the shape of open vaginas on the wet cheeks of incoming students. Asked who among them were ever caught red-handed. We grew more rebellious under our sheaths of lethargy. We sabotaged track and field events with competing schools. After graduation, we committed insidious crimes with a light touch and a good pen knife. We lifted what every straight-edge bleary-eyed sucker thought he could possess: love. We were expelled into the next life.

MELISSA McCRACKEN

Implosion

"Spontaneous combustion," he says. We're on the couch in my apartment and he is braiding, unbraiding, rebraiding my hair. I laugh. Spontaneous combustion sounds funny—calls up an image of his thin body bursting in a "poof," leaving only wispy smoke trails to drift skyward. In truth, it is probably a messy death, but I can't shake the image of him just disappearing.

He is telling me how he would like to die if he could choose. "Maybe a meteor falling on my head," he says. I think of cartoon cats crushed by space boulders that have been pulled to earth by wicked mice. The shocked look on the cats' faces just before impact always cracks me up.

I say that I want to slip away quietly in my sleep. I almost add "alone" but think better of it. I shift around on the couch, present him my feet for a massage. He says, "Front page headlines . . . blaze of glory . . . infamy."

I shake the braid from my hair, toss my head, tease him with the wordless promise of hair in his eyes, across his chest, in his mouth. "How about implosion?" I ask, which I immediately regret. I already know that he will die of a broken heart.

MELISSA McCRACKEN

It Would've Been Hot

The first and only night he and I had sex his apartment building burned down and though the "official" cause was 2B's hotplate, I wanted to blame him as I huddled in his winter coat and boxer shorts beside the fire truck—blame him because he'd been reckless and impatient, hadn't used a condom or even the couch, instead mauling me in his hallway, all long before I said, "Do you *smell* that?" and he threw open the front door, drowning us in choking smoke before he slammed it shut, coughing, and I tried to yell "back stairs" but I couldn't breathe, yet I saw him reach up with the flat of his palm and place it against the now-closed door (like in those old school-safety films) just to see, had he bothered, if it would've been hot—the same way he reached out, as the firemen pulled away, and placed his hand against the small of my back in a gesture I guess was meant to be tender but instead was after the fact.

RANDALL BROWN

Cadge

They borrow things from her—not just dye-free Tide, the organic jumbo brown eggs, a cupful of lactose-free milk. They borrow her brown Coach bag, her Barbara Heinrich pearl-gold bracelet, her Donald Pliner shoes, her Jane Bohan ring, her black Prada dress, her Infiniti G35, her pool for birthday parties, her house for the meet-and-greet for parents of new students. They borrow her wireless Internet access, two feet of the south property line, the occasional Sunday paper. At one time, they borrowed her social security number, her Platinum American Express, her CAP account.

They borrow her husband. They fly him to Cleveland, Dallas, Palm Springs, Atlanta, Boston. They borrow him for dinner, for Saturday meetings, for Sunday golf with clients flying in from Japan, India, California, skiing in Tahoe with the attorneys from Frisco. They borrow his easygoing charm, that fierce determination for that thing beyond the thing he has.

Take them, she tells them. I don't want them back. She takes longer and longer walks, farther and farther from home. She imagines the notes posted on her front door.

There must be more, one of the notes will say. And a note from her husband.

Long ago, he knocked on her apartment door, she answered with "What do you want?"—and found him and his wrinkled bow tie. "Twenty-seven times," he said. She stood behind him, on tiptoes, with no idea how to tie it, but the first try—voila! Wrapped like a present. At the wedding, it began. Her father said, "I need to borrow him for a moment." How far that moment has stretched, continues to expand.

Her husband's note could say Missed you! But it won't. I'm missing something, it'll tell her. She'll come home to find out what's gone, the something her husband can no longer name.

THERESA WYATT

Gettysburg, July, 1863

One soldier took a bullet which shattered his femur. The next day he woke up in a cellar with a woman leaning over him picking wax from his beard. She apologized, said the doctor needed light to amputate in the dark. Candles melted down to nothing were stuck everywhere, even in her bonnet.

STACE BUDZKO

How to Set a House on Fire

Before you light the gas, light a cigarette under the old red maple in the front yard, under a hunter's moon, and take a last look. Before this, walk through the ranch house with a miner's lamp and pesticide sprayer topped off with high-test racing fuel. Before it was your house it was your father's house and before it was your father's house it was his father's too. Before foreclosure on the family farm, before the new highway. Spray the gaps in the oak floorboards and get in the heating ducts, hit the horsehair plaster and take out electric sockets, then run a heavy gas line out to the barn. There is the combine. That is a backhoe. At one time chickens lived here. Before leaving, make sure the hay bales drip with fuel. This was feed once. On your way toss your house keys into the water well. Before doing anything, make a wish.

After filling the birdbath next to the old red maple with the remaining octane call Herm up at the fire station. After he gets on the line tell him to come over and bring a truck or two—with crew. There's not much to see now, really. After he asks why, tell him. Say how the fire line went from where you stand to the well and then zigzagged to the barn and after the farm equipment blew to the sky tell him how the furnace did the same. A chain of events, explain, it was a chain of events. After the windows kicked out there wasn't much anyone could have done. And after Herm asks if you would do it all over again, tell him you would. But come anyway, Herm. Tell him that.

ZACHARY SCHOMBURG

Death Letter

I get a letter in the morning that said the woman I love is dead, that she has been trampled by elephants. I haven't seen her in years, but I think about her every time I make the bed, every time I set the table. I think about how perfect we would have been together. When I arrive at her house with flowers to pay my respects, I see her in the window, dusting the sill. She isn't dead at all. She shows no signs of being trampled, even her clothes are starched and pressed. I knock on the door and she opens it. *You're not dead*, I say. *Who are you?* she says. *What do you mean?* I say. *It's me.* But her eyes just squint at me as if I were microscopic. *Weren't you trampled by elephants?* I say. *No*, she says. *There aren't even any elephants around here.* When I walk away, flowers in my fist, I think about all the different kinds of death. I wish she would have been dead just like the letter said. There is more truth in that kind of death, and I felt so much closer to her then.

DAWN RAFFEL

Near Taurus

After the rains had come and gone, we went down by the reservoir. No one was watching, or so it looked to us.

The night was like to drown us.

Our voices were high—his, mine; soft, bright—and this was not the all of it (when is it ever?).

Damp in the palm, unauthorized, young: we would never be caught, let alone apprehended, one by the other.

"Orion, over there." He was misunderstood; that's what the boy told me. "Only the belt. The body won't show until winter," he said. "Arms and such."

Me, I could not find the belt, not to save my life, I said.

Flattened with want: "There is always another time," he said.

He died, that boy. Light years! And here I am: a mother, witness, a raiser of a boy.

I could tell you his name.

I could and would not.

"Here's where the world begins," he said. I see him now—unbroken still; our naked eyes turning to legends, the dirt beneath us parched.

DAWN RAFFEL

Cheaters

In the book of the night, the man and woman sleep and oversleep until the night turns to evening. They wake to the dusk. The covers are tattered, shabby. The spine is worse for wear. Whole chapters are ragged, sticky, yellowed, and fragile from touch. The woman sighs. "We are not on the same page," she says. The man does not hear, or else does not answer, as if he is someplace far from her. Significant objects fill up the bedroom: photos, keepsakes, the earrings on the dresser, the slip on the floor. These are cherished possessions indicative of character, personal quirks. "Must you?" he says. The dusk, the woman thinks, grows thicker as she rises. Outside the window the world is gone. Nevertheless, she is yanking on garments: skirt and blouse of salient label, the bracelet he gave her, clasping clasps. The man is still groggy and speaks through a yawn. "What is the conflict now?" he says. The woman turns. Space breaks between them. The phone starts to ring, and rings through a chapter. Neither one answers. He kindles the lamp. Paragraphs spill out unvoiced: languid suspicions; an episode from childhood; a false sense of self; a shadow, if ever so faint, of hope. He watches her leaving, dressed for the day. "You'll be back," he says, as if skipping ahead, as he sinks beneath covers.

MATT SAILOR

Taste

"He doesn't have a sense of taste," Hillary said. He didn't care what we put in his sandwich—roast beef, smoked turkey, mortadella. It was all the same to him. Handfuls of mush.

He'd been coming in for a few weeks before I ever took his order. "I know just the thing," I told him, and I asked Enrique to fill his sandwich with cooked shrimp—tails, shells, heads, legs.

"It's unreal," he said, an antenna poking out of the corner of his mouth, "the texture."

The next day it was eggshells, ground down into shrapnel and sprinkled over the mayonnaise that we spread on his toasted pumpernickel.

The day after that, apple peels and orange pips—I could hear them popping as he ground them between his molars. "The best I've ever had," he told me, sliding a fifty into the tip jar.

How could I keep it up? The kitchen had only so many options. I climbed a tree behind my apartment, ground acorns down into powder. I scooped a handful of confetti from the paper shredder in the back office.

Nothing sated him—or everything did. "What do you have for me today?" he asked one Sunday in the fall. I slipped into the bathroom, sheared away locks of my hair with a carving knife.

"It'll grow back," Hillary said afterward, dropping his plate into the sink. He'd eaten every bite.

MATT SAILOR

Sea Air

Dad was on furlough that whole summer, so the only vacation we could afford was the beach.

Mom seemed concerned—was it safe? But it had been a hard year and I could see it in her eyes. She needed a break.

"You don't want to go there," said Mickey, a boy in my Algebra class who used to pull my hair at recess. "There's still people underneath. At night they walk the coast." His family was headed to the mountains like everyone else, to ski on synthetic snow.

We stayed at a Radisson that had been in the distant suburbs before the rise. It wasn't safe to swim—high Atlantic winds were sending debris in on the tides. So we stood on the balcony, watching the surf crash and break against the foundations of demolished houses. On clear days you could see the tops of drowned buildings on the horizon, where the city had been.

Our last night, I took Dad's bird-watching binoculars out on the balcony. I couldn't sleep. I couldn't stop thinking of rooms full of water, bodies trapped inside, bloated and blue.

Out in the surf, wading knee deep in the water, I saw a man. Soaking wet, pacing back and forth, his hands dead at his sides. I couldn't make out his face. But I was sure. I opened the door to Mom and Dad's adjoining room. Mom slept quietly, alone. Where Dad had been, nothing. A tangle of disturbed sheets.

SOPHIE ROSENBLUM

Once We Left Tampa

Before the sun starts to set, we're doing the foxtrot in deep water because the airline did what it wasn't supposed to do and had us surfing waves instead of clouds. Going down, I thought about the morsel of granola bar I left on the stove. If I don't make it home before the mice smell it, they'll take over, and when I get back to my place, they'll be crawling across my pillows, nesting in the crotch of my panties.

I can see the plane bobbing slowly, a metal island, the yellow raft flopping out like a tongue. I try to guess where I was sitting. I list the things in my bag still shelved overhead.

One of the flight attendants is nodding near me. She has on a manic grin, her bun soppy with ocean, brown eyes still sparkling like spun sugar, and she calls out, "We're looking for flares!" This makes me laugh because in high school there was a drama club that we made fun of called The Flairs. The guy to my left is picking at his earlobe, getting it red, and I'm thinking about his feet having to kick harder to keep him balanced.

"Don't," I want to say, but I'm not wired to reach out like that.

SOPHIE ROSENBLUM

You Sure Look Nice in This Light

It would have been strange for the hooker to wake me with a spoonful of vanilla yogurt and mashed bananas, cooing, "Wake up, sleepyhead," the way my mom used to, but I wanted it anyway. Sure, we were in a car parked at least ten miles from the closest fridge, but she might have had something in her purse to tide me over into lunch—a Jolly Rancher or gum, even. I worked hard at a job I hated, made my way through starched meetings filled with continental hellos, and then stayed nights with a small-fingered wife until I had to do it all again.

The hooker was in flats, which I knew were for running in case I was a freak or a cop or something. You'd think by now she could pinpoint the cops, spoon-smooth bald, tight in their space even on empty stretches of highway. The freaks, I could never guess. One before me, she said, looked normal enough, but wanted her to pinch the bottoms of his feet. Said it reminded him of beachside summers spent in search of mollusks with his mother. I'd said, "A real sicko," but in truth, when she'd told me, my eyes got kind of soggy at the thought.

JAMES TATE

Long-Term Memory

I was sitting in the park feeding pigeons when a man came over to me and scrutinized my face right up close. "There's a statue of you over there," he said. "You should be dead. What did you do to deserve a statue?" "I've never seen a statue of me," I said. "There can't be a statue of me. I've never done anything to deserve a statue. And I'm definitely not dead." "Well, go look for yourself. It's you alright, there's no mistaking that," he said. I got up and walked over where it was. It was me alright. I looked like I was gazing off into the distance, or the future, like those statues of pioneers. It didn't have my name on it or anything, but it was me. A lady came up to me and said, "You're looking at your own statue. Isn't that against the law, or something?" "It should be," I said, "but this is my first offense. Maybe they'll let me off light." "It's against nature, too," she said, "and bad manners, I think." "I couldn't agree with you more," I said. "I'm walking away right now, sorry." I went back to my bench. The man was sitting there. "Maybe you're a war hero. Maybe you died in the war," he said. "Never been a soldier," I said. "Maybe you founded this town three hundred years ago," he said. "Well, if I did, I don't remember it now," I said. "That's a long time ago," he said, "you coulda forgot." I went back to feeding the pigeons. Oh, yes, founding the town. It was coming back to me now. It was on a Wednesday. A light rain, my horse slowed . . .

ANA MARÍA SHUA

Hermit

With the population now well aware of the physical and mental benefits of asceticism (low cholesterol, bradycardia, a delicate sense of happiness, spiritual fulfillment), everyone wants to become a hermit. Children pretend to be Robinson Crusoe, and adolescents (stirred by their own impetus for sacrifice) prepare themselves for a life of solitude.

Men (and women too) abandon their villages (and cities) to search for desert or jungle environments, inhospitable places that have rarely if ever been trod upon, places that in practice are increasingly hard to find. The extreme scarcity of truly solitary places requires that the hermits negotiate and delineate the boundaries of their Isolation Zones, which in some cases are reduced to only a few meters around each hermitage.

This proliferation of hermits, which has ultimately altered the countryside, entices a horde of tourists. Excursions are organized to the forests where, in exchange for a large sum, the tourists can dress up in filthy sheepskins, fortify themselves with mushrooms and berries, and sleep in deliberately uncomfortable caves or huts. Before returning home, they purchase souvenirs—handcrafted objects made of roots and properly authenticated. (Although the poorer tourists, as always, make do with hot dogs and plastic imitations.)

The real hermits aren't happy about the situation, but the very traits of their vocation preclude them from acting collectively. Unsuccessful and disappointed, many return to their own villages or cities, where they reunite with their families and lead cheerful, ordinary lives until they get old, and with old age they discover the most intense solitude, except now they don't want it anymore.

LOUIS JENKINS

The Skiff

Jim was at the tiller holding her into the wind, moving us along
while I lifted the net. Then we began to drift. The net was damn
near to pull my arms off and I thought damnit Jim, pay attention to
what the hell you're doing. I turned my head to yell at him and he
wasn't there! I dropped the net, scrambled back past the engine com-
partment and grabbed the tiller, all the while looking around like
crazy to see if I could spot Jim's head above the waves . . . but there
was nothing, not even a gull, just a few clouds far away on the east-
ern horizon. I circled back along the net yelling my head off. I cut
the engine to listen. The quiet was strange after the engine noise, the
sound of the waves lapping against the hull. Not much of a wind, two-
foot waves, just a breeze out of the southwest. It seemed impossible. I
must have spent hours going around in circles, calling out, even after
I knew it was useless. There was nothing, no sign. Nothing but water

and sky. It must have been the water took him, but for all I know it was the sky. Then I noticed the half peanut butter sandwich on the seat beside me. It startled me as if it had been a snake. There was a bite out of one end. Jim's jacket was gone. That sandwich was the only thing to prove Jim had ever been here at all.

LOUIS JENKINS

Indecision

People died or moved away and did not return. Things broke and were not replaced. At one time he had owned a car and a telephone. No more. And yet somehow, things did not become more simple. Then one night, roused from sleep he stepped out naked into the below zero winter night, into the clear midnight and 20 billion stars. Nothing stirred, not a leaf, nothing out there, not the animal self, not the bird-brained self. Not a breath of wind yet somehow the door slammed shut locking behind him and knocking the kerosene lantern to the floor. Suddenly the whole place was afire. What to do? Should he try to make the mile-long run through the woods over hard-crusted snow to the nearest neighbor or just stick close to his own fire and hope that someone would see the light? The cabin was going fast. Flames leaped high above the bare trees.

CURTIS SMITH

The Storm

The siren sent the children scrambling into the hallway. They sat as they'd been taught—knees up, bowed heads covered by their hands. The lights flickered and died. In the darkness, a boy cried for his mother. A large window at the hallway's end, a frame for a purple sky veined with lightning. A crack of thunder so loud they cowered beneath its boom. More cries for mothers and fathers. The whispering of prayers. Playground mulch pelted the window, a few specks at first, then steadier, harder. Another flash, the sizzle of split air, the charge felt on the back of every neck. The wind shrieked, and the pitch escalated until it swallowed the teacher's screams for everyone to stay down. Through the window, they watched the roof of the custodian's shed lift and tumble across the baseball field.

The large boy from the special class at the end of the hallway stood. He shook off the teachers who tried to make him sit. He was like that, mute for the most part, content in his cut-off world until he exploded in fists and tears. The large boy sucked a high-diver's breath and screamed. To the children, he was a window's midday black. His wail swelled, a coiling that rose from his ribcage and gut, a cry culled from a reservoir of fear the others were only now understanding. The boy howled until he dropped, gasping, to his knees. The hallway window shattered, and in the next second, outside and in changed places. •

CURTIS SMITH

The Quarry

The young man plummets through the darkness. He crosses his ankles and cups his crotch. He closes his eyes, his world reduced to whistling air, the throb of his pulse. The shock of water striking his bare feet rides through him. Knees, hip, spine—every bony part registers the impact, a sharing of pain and exhilaration. He knifes downward, the quarry water cooler by the inch. Gravity yields to buoyancy. He opens his eyes into a different darkness. With a fluttering kick, he follows the path of bubbles. He breaks the surface and sucks in the honeysuckled air. He swims to the cliff's sheer rock and latches onto a scar cut by men long dead.

A woman's voice: "You OK?" Her words echo off the stone walls.

"I'm good," he answers.

He gazes up. A shadowed form falls from the stars. She is his brother's girl. She doesn't know about the letters that come from halfway around the world and their boastful stories of army nurses and local girls. The young man loves his brother's girl with a devotion silent and strong. The girl nears him. How appropriate, her framing amidst the quarry's backdrop, a space mysterious and beautiful and dark, its depths littered with secrets.

She hits the water, a plumb symmetry, her feet pressed together, her long hair trailing above her head. A plume rises, and the droplets rain over the young man. The stirred current pushes against his belly. For a moment, his only company is the splash's echo, the rippling surface, the mute stars. He understands a submerged object has only two options—to sink and disappear or to rise to the surface.

MARY MILLER

A Detached Observer

get off work early and go over to his house. He's out back in the dark with a pair of binoculars in his lap. "Stars pulse," he says. "Planets don't. That's how you can tell them apart." From down here everything seems to pulse but I don't say that. He has recently discovered how far away the sun is, how fucking far away, or maybe he knew all along but didn't care before.

"Let's swim," he says.

We strip off our clothes, bound down the steps and into the pool. I grab onto the diving board and pull myself up, but it doesn't matter that I'm beautiful, doesn't change the way he sees me.

"Nice tits," he says.

"I'd fuck me," I say. Then I do flips until I'm dizzy. I untuck myself and float on my back while the stars crawl across the sky and the world straightens itself back out. He gets out of the pool, jogs up the steps and into the house. He stays gone for a few minutes, plenty of time to make a phone call, for instance, and returns with a pint of whiskey.

"You try too hard," he says, sitting on the steps in the shallow end, his penis bobbing in the water like a cork. He takes a hard pull as if this distance is my fault. I don't say anything because I can't think of any way to win this conversation and there is certainly no way for me to win him, so I swim butterfly from one end of the pool to the other, displacing as much water as I can, while he watches me.

MARY MILLER

Los Angeles

The whole time I was manipulating him I was telling him how it was done.

I took the phone into the bathroom so he could hear me pee.

"I'm peeing," I said.

"Oh!" he said, "you are?"

"I had to go. By the way this is called feigned intimacy, and men love it." I told him the other ways it could be accomplished: drinking out of a man's glass, touching his knee. The whole point is early, you have to get there early.

He was far away. We'd met over the internet. It was all pretend so you could say anything. I proceeded to get drunk and tell him my problems, all the while telling him it was bad manners to get shit-faced and spill your guts right away. "Of course," I said, "my manners were never very good." I could swear I was lying but everything I said was true. He said he was Superman, took it back. What he meant was he was good in bed. I needed something to think about at night, my husband curled into the television set and a stack of books I'd never read. He'd seen pictures: contact lenses, mascara, looking away from the camera.

"I'm pretty," I said, giving him my bra size.

"I know you're pretty!" he said. "You're hot! And D-cups don't hurt either!" He called out for Jesus then. I felt bugs crawling on my face but there was nothing there.

I was looking for a way out. Once I found it I would find my way back in. I didn't know where he was coming from. He lived in Los Angeles, palm trees out his window.

DON SHEA

Blindsided

I t started as a low, sweet jumble of sound, whiny and country, from
the far end of the subway car. Then you could make out a small, pale
man of middle years and thinning hair shuffling forward through the
passengers with a dog by his side and a sack on his back containing a
radio or tape player from which this strangely sweet country sound—
a voice, a guitar and fiddle—was spilling out and he was singing
along with it, singing along with his own voice or whoever's, singing
softly in a nasal tenor as clear as spring water, and then you recognized the song, one of John Denver's impossibly sentimental ballads
about home and hearth and supper on the stove that you were always
ashamed of liking, but you would not be taken that easily—street-
smart New Yorker—and you searched his bowed head for fraud,
searched out his eyes even as you reached for your loose change, and
just then the small pale man drew abreast of you and threw back his

head, and as his eyes came up milky and twisted and wrong, his face fused ecstatically and the purest sound came forth from him and struck something inside you that came undone, and you would have given great value at that moment to see what he saw, to see what lay beyond embarrassment.

RICHARD BRAUTIGAN

Women When They Put Their Clothes On in the Morning

It's really a very beautiful exchange of values when women put their clothes on in the morning and she is brand-new and you've never seen her put her clothes on before.

You've been lovers and you've slept together and there's nothing more you can do about that, so it's time for her to put her clothes on.

Maybe you've already had breakfast and she's slipped her sweater on to cook a nice bare-assed breakfast for you, padding in sweet flesh around the kitchen, and you both discussed in length the poetry of Rilke which she knew a great deal about, surprising you.

But now it's time for her to put her clothes on because you've both had so much coffee that you can't drink any more and it's time for her to go home and it's time for her to go to work and you want to stay there alone because you've got some things to do around the house and you're going outside together for a nice walk and it's time for *you* to go home and it's time for *you* to go to work and she's got some things that she wants to do around the house.

Or . . . maybe it's even love.

But anyway: It's time for her to put her clothes on and it's so beautiful when she does it. Her body slowly disappears and comes out quite nicely all in clothes. There's a virginal quality to it. She's got her clothes on, and the beginning is over.

TARA LYNN MASIH

This Heat

Bats are flying around on the third floor again. Trapped. We live on a hill, so the height attracts them. Like a belfry. My husband is gone again. The beans he planted in the garden during the full moon are wilting. I'm not tending to the new shoots in this July heat. Like the jungle, he says, this heat. The news is bad lately. More troops killed this month than in any other. I keep the paper away from him, but he watches the reports on TV. This new war brings the old one back. In his sleep, he fights with the chain that hangs from the overhead bedroom light. He is always waging some past battle. Sometimes his hands find my throat. He leaves after these episodes. To be alone. At least he doesn't wander the streets, like some. Doesn't get lost permanently. He always comes back. Till then, I live with the bats. They flutter their wings of skin against the screens, while I lie in bed, staring up at the ghost of a light.

TARA LYNN MASIH

Ella

ELLA: THEN

Ella likes things tiny. Tiny toy dishes, tiny dolls, tiny flowers. She even wants her dad to be tiny. Like the *Incredible Shrinking Man* she saw on the telly. He could live in her Lincoln Log Cabin. She would feed him a green pea on her tiny doll's plate for supper.

Ella has a tiny pet. From her dad's Ronson cigarette lighter, a flint. Red. Blowing the cylinder bead gently across the floor, she is taking it for a walk. It lives in a matchbox with tissue sheets and clover. Till it falls in a canyon between floorboards. He won't give her another.

Ella's father does not shrink to a point of control. He smokes, stares, strokes, rolls her around. She goes tiny and red to disappear in cracks.

ELLA: NOW

Ella spends too much time in bars these days. Neon light from Budweiser and Michelob beer signs washes over her. Different colors, depending on where you sit.

Ella is known for this small trick—she sits the flat end of a cigarette butt down on the bar top, so the tobacco burns on its own. She drinks more than smokes. The vapors curling up into the red-green neon haze. The live embers evolving into columns of cold ash. If someone breathes too hard, they collapse.

She strikes another match, then another, till five butts form a circle like Stonehenge . . . gray . . . silent. This reminds her of something she can't quite hold on to when she wanders home, outside air black and stifling.

Her pastor once told her, transformation requires inspiration. She has forgotten.

RON CARLSON

Grief

The King died. Long live the King. And then the Queen died. She was buried beside him. The King died and then the Queen died of grief. This was the posted report. And no one said a thing. But you can't die of grief. It can take away your appetite and keep you in your chamber, but not forever. It isn't terminal. Eventually you'll come out and want a toddy. The Queen died subsequent to the King, but not of grief. I know the royal coroner, have seen him around, a young guy with a good job. The death rate for the royalty is so much lower than that of the general populace. He was summoned by the musicians, found her on the bedroom floor, checked for a pulse, and wrote "Grief" on the form. It looked good. And it was necessary. It answered the thousand questions about the state of the nation. He didn't examine the body, perform an autopsy. If he had, he wouldn't have found grief. There is no place for grief in the body. He would have found a blood alcohol level of point one nine and he would have found a clot of improperly chewed tangerine in the lady's throat which she had ingested while laughing. But this seems a fine point. The Queen is dead. Long live her grief. Long live the Duke of Reddington and the Earl of Halstar who were with me that night entertaining the Queen in her chambers. She was a vigorous sort. And long live the posted report which will always fill a royal place in this old kingdom.

AFTERWORD

Readers of *New Micro* may wonder what distinguishes these exceptionally short fictions from prose poems, since they occupy the same amount of space and employ similar means of address—sketch, parable, anecdote, fable, joke, letter, meditation, and so on. The classic test for telling the difference between fiction writers and poets at a cocktail party—fiction writers talk contracts, and agents, and money, while poets talk food—may not apply to those who call it a day at 300 words. No one gets rich writing micros.

Less is more: this is the currency of prose poetry and microfiction alike. They also share a border—the sentence—that from either side is subject to continual dispute and change. (The small wars of the literati never end.) Is this a prose poem or a micro? It hardly matters. Literary guides to uncertain terrain, this no-man's-land, are always getting lost. Better to follow the intrepid explorers included in this anthology who navigate that border with exquisite care, distilling in exacting prose new ways of reading the world.

What have we here? A fable in the form of a news dispatch about a drive-by shooting. A portrait of a woman whose burning misery is, in her words, "the mystery of the incongruous." A love story, and then another. Someone's heart is breaking. Someone is taking dictation from the stars. A story begins to take shape. Listen closely. It will not last long, but it will haunt you forever.

—Christopher Merrill

ACKNOWLEDGMENTS

We would like to thank our editor, Amy Cherry, for her steady guidance; Margaret Gorenstein, our invaluable permissions consultant; and Nat Sobel, our agent, for making the connections. Thanks also to our close associates who saw us all the way through and made all the difference: Diana Scott, Andrew Root, Denise Robinow, and Ron & Renee Geyer. And finally, enormous thanks to Pamela Painter and Meg Pokrass, who were there at the beginning.

BOOKS by the AUTHORS

The source books for the stories in *New Micro* are listed here first, followed by a selection of the authors' other books, from newest to oldest.

Kim Addonizio: *Jimmy & Rita* (Stephen F. Austin University Press, 2012); *Mortal Trash* (W. W. Norton, 2016); *Bukowski in a Sundress* (Penguin, 2016); *The Palace of Illusions* (Soft Skull Press, 2014).

Roberta Allen: *Certain People* (Coffee House Press, 1996); *The Princess of Herself* (Pelekinesis, 2017); *The Dreaming Girl* (Ellipsis Press, 2011); *Amazon Dream* (City Lights Publishers, 1992).

Steve Almond: *This Won't Take But a Minute, Honey* (DIY or DIE Press, 2010); *God Bless America* (Lookout Books, 2011); *Rock and Roll Will Save Your Life* (Random House, 2010); *The Evil B. B. Chow* (Algonquin Books, 2005).

Nin Andrews: *Our Lady of the Orgasm* (MadHat Press, 2017); *Miss August* (Cavenkerry, 2017); *Why God Is a Woman* (BOA Editions, 2015); *Sleeping with Houdini* (BOA Editions, 2008); *Midlife Crisis with Dick and Jane* (Web del Sol, 2005).

Arlene Ang: *Banned for Life* (Misty Publications, 2014); *Seeing Birds in Church Is a Kind of Adieu* (Cinnamon Press, 2010); *The Desecration of Doves* (iUniverse, 2005).

Barry Basden: *Used Rainbow* (Red Dashboard, 2014); *Wince* (Camroc Press, 2015).

Lou Beach: *420 Characters* (Houghton Mifflin Harcourt, 2011); *Cut It Out* (Last Gasp, 2015).

Paul Beckman: *Peek* (Big Table Publishing Company, 2014); *Maybe I Ought to Sit Quietly in a Dark Room for a While* (Amazon Digital Services, 2013); *Come, Meet My Family* (Small Press Distribution, 1997).

Richard Brautigan: *Revenge of the Lawn* (Simon & Schuster, 1971); *In Watermelon Sugar* (Four Seasons Foundation, 1968); *Trout Fishing in America* (Four Seasons Foundation, 1967); *A Confederate General from Big Sur* (Grove Press, 1964).

Randall Brown: *Mad to Live* (Flume Press, 2008); *A Pocket Guide to Flash Fiction* (Matter Press, 2012).

Bonnie Jo Campbell: *Mothers, Tell Your Daughters* (W. W. Norton, 2015); *Once Upon a River* (W. W. Norton, 2012); *American Salvage* (W. W. Norton, 2009); *Women & Other Animals* (Scribner, 2002).

Ron Carlson: *Room Service* (Red Hen Press, 2012); *The Blue Box* (Red Hen Press, 2014); *Return to Oakpine* (Viking, 2013); *Five Skies* (Viking, 2007).

Kim Chinquee: *Pretty* (White Pine Press, 2010); *Veer* (Ravenna Press, 2017); *Oh Baby* (Ravenna Press, 2008).

James Claffey: *Blood a Cold Blue* (Press 53, 2013).

Amy L. Clark: *Wanting* appears in *A Peculiar Feeling of Restlessness* (Rose Metal Press, 2008); *Adulterous Generation* (Queen's Ferry Press, 2016).

Bernard Cooper: *Maps to Anywhere* (University of Georgia Press, 1997); *My Avant-Garde Education* (W. W. Norton, 2015); *The Bill from My Father* (Simon & Schuster, 2007); *Guess Again* (Simon & Schuster, 2006).

Michael Czyzniejewski: *Chicago Stories* (Curbside Splendor, 2012); *I Will Love You for the Rest of My Life* (Curbside Splendor, 2015); *Elephants in Our Bedroom* (Dzanc Books, 2009).

Gay Degani: *Rattle of Want* (Pure Slush Books, 2015); *What Came Before* (Every Day Novels, 2014); *Pomegranate Stories* (lulu.com, 2010).

Erin Dionne: *Notes from an Accidental Band Geek* (Puffin Books, 2012); *The Total Tragedy of a Girl Named Hamlet* (Puffin Books, 2011); *Models Don't Eat Chocolate Cookies* (Dial Books, 2009).

Stuart Dybek: *Ecstatic Cahoots* (Farrar, Straus and Giroux, 2014); *Paper Lantern* (Farrar, Straus and Giroux, 2014); *Streets in Their Own Ink* (Farrar, Straus, and Giroux, 2006); *I Sailed with Magellan* (Farrar, Straus, and Giroux, 2003).

Pia Z. Ehrhardt: *Famous Fathers & Other Stories* (MacAdam/Cage, 2007).

Elizabeth Ellen: *Sixteen Miles Outside of Phoenix* appears in *A Peculiar Feeling of Restlessness* (Rose Metal Press, 2008); *Person/a* (Short Flight/Long Drive Books, 2017); *Bridget Fonda* (Dostoyevsky Wannabe, 2015); *Fast Machine* (Short Flight/Long Drive, 2012).

Grant Faulkner: *Fissures: One Hundred 100-Word Stories* (Press 53, 2015); *Pep Talks for Writers* (Chronicle Books, 2017).

Kathy Fish: *Rift* (Unknown Press, 2011); *Wild Life* (Matter Press, 2011); *Laughter, Applause, Laughter, Music, Applause* appeared in *A Peculiar Feeling of Restlessness* (Rose Metal Press, 2008).

Sherrie Flick: *Whiskey, Etc.* (Autumn House, 2017); *Reconsidering Happiness* (Bison Books, 2009); *I Call This Flirting* (Flume Press, 2004).

Thaisa Frank: *Enchantment* (Counterpoint, 2012); *Heidegger's Glasses* (Counterpoint, 2011); *Finding Your Writer's Voice* (St. Martin's

Griffin, 1996); *A Brief History of Camouflage* (Black Sparrow Press, 1992).

Melissa Fraterrigo: *Glory Days* (University of Nebraska Press, 2017); *The Longest Pregnancy* (Livingston Press, 2011).

Stefanie Freele: *Feeding Strays* (Lost Horse Press, 2009); *Surrounded by Water* (Press 53, 2012).

Sarah Freligh: *Sad Math* (Moon City Press, 2015); *A Brief Natural History of an American Girl* (Accents Publishing, 2012); *Sort of Gone* (Turning Point, 2008).

Molly Giles: *Bothered* (Split Oak Press, 2012); *All the Wrong Places* (Lost Horse Press, 2015); *Rough Translations* (University of Georgia Press, 2004); *Iron Shoes* (Simon & Schuster, 2001).

Amelia Gray: *AM/PM* (Featherproof Books, 2009); *Isadora* (Farrar, Straus and Giroux, 2017); *Gutshot* (Farrar, Straus and Giroux, 2015); *Museum of the Weird* (Fiction Collective, 2010).

Kevin Griffith: *Denmark, Kangaroo, Orange* (Pearl Editions, 2008); *101 Kinds of Irony* (Folded Word, 2012); *Paradise Refunded* (Backwaters Press, 1998).

Tom Hazuka: *You Have Time for This* (Ooligan Press, 2007); *Flash Fiction Funny* (Bluelight Press, 2013); *Sudden Flash Youth* (Persea, 2011); *A Celestial Omnibus* (Beacon Press, 1998).

Kyle Hemmings: *Split Brain* (CreateSpace, 2016); *You Never Die in Wholes* (Good Story Press, 2012).

Amy Hempel: *Reasons to Live* (HarperPerennial, 1995); *The Dog of the Marriage* (Scribner, 2005); *At the Gates of the Animal Kingdom* (Knopf, 1990).

Tania Hershman: *My Mother Was an Upright Piano* (Tangent Books, 2012); *Some of Us Glow More Than Others* (Unthank Books, 2017); *Terms and Conditions* (Nine Arches Press, 2017); *Writing Short Stories: A Writers' and Artists' Companion* (Bloomsbury, 2014).

Jim Heynen: *Why Would a Woman Pour Boiling Water on Her Head?* (Trilobite Press, 2001); *Ordinary Sins* (Milkweed Editions, 2014);

The Fall of Alice K. (Milkweed Editions, 2012); *The One-Room Schoolhouse* (Knopf, 1993).

Tiff Holland: *Betty Superman* (Rose Metal Press, 2011).

Louis Jenkins: *Just Above Water* (Holy Cow! Press, 1999); *In the Sun Out of the Wind* (Will o' the Wisp Press, 2017); *Tin Flag* (Will o' the Wisp Books, 2013); *Before You Know It* (Will o' the Wisp Books, 2009).

Roy Kesey: *All Over* (Dzanc Books, 2007); *Any Deadly Thing* (Dzanc Books, 2013); *Pacazo* (Dzanc Books, 2011); *Nothing in the World* (Dzanc Books, 2008).

Ron Koertge: *Sex World* (Red Hen Press, 2014); *Vampire Planet* (Red Hen Press, 2016); *Coaltown Jesus* (Candlewick, 2013); *Lies, Knives, and Girls in Red Dresses* (Candlewick, 2012).

Len Kuntz: *I'm Not Supposed to Be Here and Neither Are You* (Unknown Press, 2016).

Jeff Landon: *Truck Dance* (Matter Press, 2011); *Emily Avenue* (Fast Forward Press, 2011).

Tara Laskowski: *Modern Manners for Your Inner Demons* (Santa Fe Writer's Project, 2017); *Bystanders* (Santa Fe Writer's Project, 2016); *SmokeLong: The Best of the First Ten Years* (Matter Press, 2014).

Lorraine López: *The Realm of Happy Spirits* (Grand Central Publishing, 2011); *Homicide Survivors Picnic* (BkMk Press, 2009); *The Gifted Gabaldón Sisters* (Grand Central Publishing, 2008).

Debra Marquart: *The Hunger Bone: Rock & Roll Stories* (New Rivers Press, 2001); *Small Buried Things* (New Rivers Press, 2015); *From Sweetness* (Pearl Editions, 2001); *Everything's a Verb* (New Rivers Press, 1995).

Michael Martone: *Memoranda* (Bull City Press, 2015); *Double-wide* (Quarry Books, 2007); *Michael Martone* (Fiction Collective, 2005); *Blue Guide to Indiana* (Fiction Collective, 2001).

Tara Lynn Masih: *Best Small Fictions* (Braddock Avenue Books,

2017, Queen's Ferry Press, 2016, 2015); *The Chalk Circle* (Wyatt-MacKenzie, 2012); *Where the Dog Star Never Glows* (Press 53, 2010); *The Rose Metal Press Field Guide to Writing Flash Fiction* (Rose Metal Press, 2009).

Kathleen McGookey: *Whatever Shines* (White Pine Press, 2001); *Heart in a Jar* (White Pine Press, 2017); *Stay* (Press 53, 2015).

Christopher Merkner: *The Rise & Fall of the Scandamerican Domestic* (Coffee House Press, 2014).

Christopher Merrill: *Self-Portrait with Dogwood* (Trinity University Press, 2017); *Flash Fiction International* (W. W. Norton, 2015); *Necessities* (White Pine Press, 2013); *Boat* (Tupelo Press, 2013).

Mary Miller: *Less Shiny* (Magic Helicopter Press, 2008); *Always Happy Hour* (Liveright, 2017); *The Last Days of California* (Liveright, 2014); *Big World* (Short Flight/Long Drive Books, 2009).

Dinty W. Moore: *The Story Cure* (Ten Speed Press, 2017); *The Mindful Writer* (Wisdom Publications, 2016); *Dear Mister Essay Writer Guy* (Ten Speed Press, 2015); *Between Panic and Desire* (Bison Books, 2010).

Darlin' Neal: *Elegant Punk* (Press 53, 2012); *Rattlesnakes & the Moon* (Press 53, 2010).

Joyce Carol Oates: *The Assignation* (Harper & Row, 1988); *A Book of Martyrs* (Ecco, 2017); *Jack of Spades* (Mysterious Press, 2015); *A Widow's Story* (Ecco, 2012).

Peter Orner: *Esther Stories* (Little Brown and Company, 2014); *Am I Here Alone* (Catapult, 2016); *Last Car Over the Sagamore Bridge* (Back Bay Books, 2014); *Love and Shame and Love* (Back Bay Books, 2012).

Pamela Painter: *Ways to Spend the Night* (Engine Books, 2016); *Wouldn't You Like to Know* (Carnegie Mellon, 2010); *Getting to Know the Weather* (Carnegie Mellon, 2008); *The Long and Short of It* (Carnegie Mellon University Press, 1999).

Jennifer Pieroni: *Danceland* (Queen's Ferry Press, 2014).

Meg Pokrass: *Damn Sure Right* (Press 53, 2011); *The Dog Looks Happy*

Upside Down (Etruscan Press, 2016); *Cellulose Pajamas* (Blue Light Press, 2015); *Here, Where We Live* appeared in *My Very End of the Universe* (Rose Metal Press, 2014).

Pedro Ponce: *Alien Autopsy* (Cow Heavy Books, 2010); *Superstitions of Apartment Life* (Burnside Review Press, 2008).

Dawn Raffel: *Further Adventures in a Restless Universe* (Dzanc Books, 2010); *The Strange Case of Dr. Couney: How a Mysterious European Showman Saved Thousands of American Babies* (Blue Rider Books, 2018); *The Secret Life of Objects* (Jaded Ibis Press, 2012); *Carrying the Body* (Scribner, 2002).

Josh Russell: *A True History of the Captivation, Transport to Strange Lands, and Deliverance of Hannah Guttentag* (Dzanc Books, 2012); *My Bright Midnight* (Louisiana State University Press, 2010); *Yellow Jack* (W. W. Norton, 2000).

Zachary Schomburg: *Fjords Vol. 1* (Black Ocean Press, 2014); *Mammother* (Featherproof Books, 2017); *The Book of Joshua* (Black Ocean, 2014); *The Man Suit* (Back Ocean, 2007).

Robert Shapard: *Flash Fiction International* (W. W. Norton, 2015); *New Sudden Fiction* (W. W. Norton, 2007); *Flash Fiction Forward* (W. W. Norton, 2006); *Motel and Other Stories* (Predator Press, 2005).

Steven Sherrill: *The Minotaur Takes His Own Sweet Time* (John F. Blair, Publisher, 2016); *The Locktender's House* (Random House, 2008); *Visits from the Drowned Girl* (Random House, 2004); *The Minotaur Takes a Cigarette Break* (Picador, 2002).

Ana María Shua: *Without a Net* (Hanging Loose Press, 2012); *The Weight of Translation* (University of Nebraska Press, 2012); *Death as a Side Effect* (Bison Books, 2010); *Microfictions* (Bison Books, 2009).

David Shumate: *High Water Mark* (University of Pittsburgh Press, 2004); *Kimonos in the Closet* (University of Pittsburgh Press, 2013); *The Floating Bridge* (University of Pittsburgh Press, 2008).

Claudia Smith: *The Sky Is a Well* appeared in *A Peculiar Feeling of*

Restlessness (Rose Metal Press, 2008); *Quarry Light* (Magic Helicopter Press, 2013); *Put Your Head in My Lap* (Future Tense Books, 2012).

Curtis Smith: *Beasts & Men* (Press 53, 2013); *In the Jukebox Light* (March Street Press, 2004).

Nancy Stohlman: *The Vixen Scream* (Pure Slush, 2014); *The Monster Opera* (Bartleby Snopes Press, 2013); *Searching for Suzi* (Monkey Puzzle Press, 2009); *Live from Palestine* (South End Press, 2003).

James Tate: *Return to the City of White Donkeys* (HarperCollins, 2004); *Dome of the Hidden Pavilion* (Ecco Press, 2015); *The Ghost Soldiers* (Ecco Press, 2008); *Memoir of the Hawk* (Ecco Press, 2002).

Anthony Tognazzini: *I Carry a Hammer in My Pocket for Occasions Such as These* (BOA Editions, 2007).

Meg Tuite: *Disparate Pathos* (Monkey Puzzle Press, 2011); *Grace Notes* (Unknown Press, 2015); *Bound by Blue* (Sententia Books, 2013); *Domestic Apparition* (San Francisco Bay Press, 2012).

Robert Vaughan: *Rift* (Unknown Press, 2015); *Funhouse* (Unknown Press, 2016); *Addicts & Basements* (Civil Coping Mechanisms, 2014).

Ron Wallace: *Quick Bright Things* (Mid-List Press, 2000); *For Dear Life* (University of Pittsburgh Press, 2015); *The Uses of Adversity* (University of Pittsburgh Press, 1998).

William Walsh: *Pathologies* (Keyhole Press, 2010); *Stephen King Stephen King* (Keyhole Press, 2016); *Ampersand, Mass.* (Keyhole Press, 2011); *Without Wax* (Casperian Books, 2008).

John Edgar Wideman: *Briefs: Stories from the Palm of the Mind* (Lulu. com, 2010); *Writing to Save a Life* (Scribner, 2016); *Philadelphia Story* (Mariner Books, 2005); *Brothers and Keepers* (Mariner Books, reprint, 2005).

Diane Williams: *Fine, Fine, Fine, Fine, Fine* (McSweeney's, 2016); *Vicky Swanky Is a Beauty* (McSweeney's, 2012); *Romancer Erector*

(Dalkey Archive Press, 2001); *Excitability* (Dalkey Archive Press, 1998).

Joy Williams: *Ninety-Nine Stories of God* (Tin House Books, 2016); *The Visiting Privilege* (Vintage, 2015); *Honored Guest* (Knopf, 2004); *The Quick and the Dead* (Vintage, 2002).

Francine Witte: *Cold June* (Ropewalk Press, 2010); *Not All Fires Burn the Same* (Slipstream, 2016); *Only, Not Only* (Finishing Line Press, 2012); *First Rain* (Pecan Grove Press, 2009).

Theresa Wyatt: *Hurled into Gettysburg* (BlazeVOX Books, 2017).

CREDITS